Secrets of a Noble

Key Keeper

- The Story of Dreamland -

This book is supplemental
to the Dandelions book.
It is the story Annabelle
created for her librarian
friend, Mr. Lundstrom.
Enjoy!

       — Richelle E. Goodrich

Secrets of a Noble

Key Keeper

- The Story of Dreamland -

as imagined
by
Miss Annabelle Fancher

Edited and amended for publication
By Richelle E. Goodrich
and Michael D. Lundstrom

For Gregory Hill
and especially Gavin

Table of Contents

There are things
that make no sense,
that seem unreal,
that can't be grasped
or understood
or explained,
that maybe don't even exist...
And still, somehow, those
wonderful things
touch and change our lives.
Isn't it strange?

—Miss Annabelle Fancher

Chapter One
The Little Boy

Never in your wildest dreams would you think it a good thing to be swallowed whole by a big bad wolf. That is, until you met Gavin. But he's an unusual boy, as you'll soon find out; one with a dizzy imagination and crazy powers and secrets no ordinary person would think to have. This includes a fascination for exploring inside the bellies of ogres and gargoyles and other scary creatures such as big bad wolves—which is exactly where this story begins. Unbelievable to you, perhaps, but quite believable to me.

It was inside the belly of a big bad hairy wolf that Gavin was roaming about, searching by flashlight for something important the beast had swallowed. Something other than himself.

"Um...are you okay down there?" someone squeaked in a loud whisper from outside. It was the frightened voice of a younger boy.

"Of course I'm okay!" came a sure answer. The response rose from the throat of the sleeping wolf, though the wolf's mouth didn't move to form any words.

Gavin spoke again from deep inside a full belly that smelled of dead fish and rotten apples. "I still don't see a truck in here—not one. Are you sure he ate it?"

"Oh, oh yes, I'm sure; I watched him swallow it whole! That big bad wolf told me he was going to eat *me* next, just like he ate my toy truck! I really do want it back; it was a gift from my Grandpapa."

"Well, I don't see it. There's a lot of other stuff down here—a soggy baseball, an empty turtle shell, some crocodile teeth, a perfectly good rabbit's foot, and a dead frog. Would you rather have one of those?"

"Oh, no, no, no! I really want my truck, please."

"Ah-ha!" The sound of success burped up from the wolf's belly. "I've found it!"

With big eyes, the hopeful little boy watched a large blob work its way through the sleeping beast, slowly maneuvering from tummy to throat. The moving blob caused the wolf's hairy back to arch and its neck to swell three times normal size. Long, skinny fingers reached out from the mouth, taking hold of a wet snout. Gavin wriggled and pulled and climbed until at last his lanky body emerged—a young but tall figure with dark brown eyes and a messy mop of curls on his head to match.

It took a moment for the little boy to get past an understandable case of shock. But soon enough his wide eyes dropped from Gavin's triumphant grin to the clunky, red fire engine held out in offer.

"My fire truck! Oh, oh thank you!" The boy ran to reclaim his precious gift. "I could never have faced my Grandpapa had I lost it. He'd be so angry with me."

Gavin shrugged casually. "It was nothing really."

"Oh, oh no!" said the boy, "It was something! You were so brave to let that wolf swallow you whole! And how clever to knock him in the head with the heel of your boot on the way down. He may have eaten *me* if you'd not come along!"

"And what fun it would've been had you been eaten!"

Gavin smiled cheerily, but the little boy failed to share the same expression.

"Oh, oh no, no, no! I don't want to be eaten! No, no, never ever!"

"And why not?"

"Well…..because it might hurt!" the boy exclaimed. His round cheeks turned red as he admitted in a small voice, "And I'm afraid of the dark."

"If that's the case, maybe you should keep a flashlight in your pocket. Then dumb old wolves couldn't frighten you and chase you up really high walls." Each boy glanced over his shoulder at a tall, white, stone barrier covered in ivy and blue blossoms. It stretched out of sight in either direction.

"I hadn't thought of that before," the little boy said, skewing his eyebrows.

Gavin presented an open palm where a small flashlight suddenly appeared.

"For me?"

"For you."

"Oh, oh thank you!"   The child repaid his giver with a tight hug around the waist.   He stepped away quickly enough, wearing a look of puzzlement on his face.   "You've been so very kind to me, and I don't even know who you are?"

The older boy lifted a pointed chin and jerked his head in a proud manner before announcing, "I am Gavin, the key keeper."

His admirer's face brightened.   The youngster was highly intrigued.   "Oh, oh, a key keeper!   And how many keys do you keep?"

"Just one."

"That's all?"

"That's all I need."

The child considered this, unsure what to ask next.   He decided to let every question in his head tumble out of his mouth at once.   "Is it a big key?   Can I see it?   Does it open everything or just one thing?   Will it open a treasure chest?   Or a hidden safe?   Or a prison cell?   Or is it meant for a door to a secret room?"

The key keeper reached into his shirt to fish out the item in question.   "Yes you may see it."   A bronze skeleton key appeared, pinched between two fingers.   The polished surface shimmered over detailed engravings.   He answered the last question.   "And, yes, you might say it opens a door...of sorts."

The boy went to touch the key, but Gavin held it out of reach.

"Oh, oh, does it unlock an important door?"

Gavin nodded assuredly, making his dark curls bounce.

"Oh, oh please, may I watch you open it?"

The key keeper took a moment to think while the smaller boy wordlessly begged with adorable, pleading eyes for the privilege to see the decorative key in use.   Gavin slipped it back beneath his shirt where it hung safely from a braided chain.   He was never without that key around his neck—both night and day.

"I suppose you could come along and help search for the right door."

"Oh, oh thank you!   Thank you!   I won't be a bother, oh, oh, I promise!"

Within a blink, everything about their surroundings changed.   The sleeping wolf, the forest, the ivy-laden wall—it all vanished, giving way to a never-ending hall of facing doors. As Gavin stepped between the closed doors, his follower kept very near.   There was no ceiling to look up at and no floor to tap a shoe against, yet the two were able to walk with ease down the peculiar corridor of shut-off entries and exits.

Sounds and fragrances as well as whiffs of sweetness strong enough to taste emanated from the doors.   Each was unique in appearance and color.   Each hid secrets on the inside.

A glossy white door with a brass ball knob appeared to swell and shrink repeatedly as if breathing in air.   Singing, soft and womanly, penetrated the painted wood.   The little boy stepped closer.   His ear perked to hear a lullaby.

"The stars can't put on a sparkly show,
The fullest moon can't reflect a glow,
The hottest sun cannot burn, you know,
Bright enough to outshine my dear child."

He stepped away easily enough, not enticed by a mother's song of admiration.

The next entry that appealed to the boy was a high, wooden set of double doors.   They were encased in arched framing.   Polished, bronze handles reached out from the center in swirled figure eights.   Behind these doors a stringed orchestra erupted into glorious music-making.   Gavin looked sideways and watched the child creep close, behaving as if tempted to steal a peek at the auditorium inside.   But the curious listener backed away without trying the handles.   He glanced back at Gavin.

"Which door will your key unlock?   I really want to know!"

The question was answered with another question. "Which door do you wish it to unlock?"

The little boy ran his eyes up both sides of the corridor, unable to decide.   He continued forward, just a couple steps in front of his guide.

They passed weathered wooden barriers from which talking, laughing, singing, and persistent begging called to them.   They passed freshly-painted doors where smells of burning apple wood, homemade pastries, and frying fish compelled a good sniff.   There were doors that thumped, doors that cried, and doors that resonated with eerie clatter. These, the lad stepped quickly past.   It was a plain, rectangular, mahogany slab of wood that made him stop in his tracks.   A simple thumb-press handle glimmered for attention on the right-hand side.

"This looks exactly like Grandpapa's...." the boy trailed off, wondering.   He stepped up and placed a hand against the dull surface.   His ear followed.   It was nearly silent on the other side except for the sound of an old man's snores.

"I think it is Grandpapa!"

There was no hesitation in his next move.   With a familiar squeeze on the knob and a light push against the wood, the door opened inward.   The little boy took a step toward his Grandfather's amplified snoring.....and disappeared.   He hadn't even thought to ask Gavin to use his special key.

"And that's that!" The key keeper smirked triumphantly. He clapped his hands once and swiveled on the balls of his feet. With his chore accomplished, he set out for home.

Now, you may be wondering what kind of gruesome chore it is to make a seemingly nice little boy disappear, but I guarantee there's no sordid mischief at play here. There are things you must understand about a key keeper. The first is that he is an honorable and noble character. Were it not so, the heads of parliament in Dreamland would come together to judge and ultimately dismiss him from his calling. Such a thing would be highly disgraceful for a key keeper! So you see, Gavin is exactly the opposite of sordid or shady in his dealings with stray dreamers.

And, oh yes, that little boy was indeed dreaming. Where else but in dreams could you be swallowed whole by a big bad hairy wolf and find it ticklish fun?

Chapter Two
Swashbucklin' Pirates

The wall that surrounds Dreamland is of unknown measure. Some find it small enough to barely fit a cozy village in its circle. Others insist a great and marvelous city exists within its boundaries, including avenues of skyscrapers surrounded by miles of two-story neighborhoods. Once, I actually sailed the ocean inside these guarded walls. You may say impossible, but not so.

I say "not so" because I know a secret. Lend me your ear and I will share it with you. But first, promise to keep the secret, for this wondrous truth must be carefully kept.

Dreamland is an actual place; it really exists!

Oh yes, yes, it truly does! And what's astonishing is how this magical world has endured forever in a realm only visible to dreamers. Hence the name, perhaps.

Bring your ear closer and I will share a better secret. This too must be protected.

Reality in Dreamland is whatever you want it to be.

The details of this enchanted world are formed in the eye of the beholder. In other words, when you step through the gates of this marvelous land, whatever you wish for becomes so. If your desire is to experience life on acres of farmland, that's exactly what you'll find. If you prefer a bustling city, such a reality will appear. If you yearn to sail the world's oceans within a gated border, it will be as you wish. And that is the big secret Gavin, the key keeper, protects.

It is his job to prevent wandering dreamers from trespassing the gates of Dreamland. For if they were to scale the wall, or tunnel beneath it, or find some way across its borders, the likelihood is great they would never choose to leave such a paradise. That fact is understandable, of course. If you could have anything you wished for—anything imaginable—would you so easily turn away from it? Would you abandon your dreams to wake up again?

It might help to see the truth in action before deciding. And what better way than to visit the magical land in question?

The hall of doors where we last left Gavin happens to end where a dark forest begins. Or possibly the hallway begins where the forest ends; I'm not quite certain. Either way, the trees in that timbered area are so congested with leafy

20

tops that barely a shard of sunlight slips through. Within the woods are hiding places that shield and shelter the most ferocious of monsters. But their introduction will be saved for another time.

Having his duties handled for the present moment, Gavin made his way through the forest toward the outside wall enclosing Dreamland. He seemed undaunted by a thick growth of ivy that nearly concealed the wall from view.

Though it appeared to be a dead end, his footsteps moved forward with confident strides, taking him right up to the wall. Slipping a hand beneath his shirt, he retrieved his key and held it in front of him like a warding symbol—as far as the attached chain would allow. As if fearful, or perhaps respectful of the power trapped within the key, the ivy and its blue blooms peeled away, opening a narrow area before the stone wall. The exposed gates glimmered as if sprinkled with pixie dust, reflecting all available light off a dimpled texture.

Depressed in the stone at shoulder height was a square groove about the size of a hand. An indentation appeared like a mold in the center of it. Gavin brought up his bronze key, behaving as if he'd performed the same move a million times, and placed it over the indentation. A perfect match! The walls began to tremble, and he stepped back, slipping the key beneath his shirt once again.

The gates parted by only a fraction and then closed behind the key keeper as soon as he stepped inside. What his eyes took in was a wondrous view of home; a world shaped to his own personal liking.

The ground looked like black crumbs—moist, rich dirt that mashed under every footstep. The soil quickly disappeared beneath plant life that crowded the landscape beyond. In every direction a wall of rainforest blocked off any decent view of the horizon. Trees towered like giants, joined together by drooping swags of moss.   Vines as thick in circumference as plumber's pipe entangled every sturdy tree branch.   The underbrush stood unusually high as well, extending up to Gavin's waist, some ferns stretching to brush their feathered fronds against his shoulders.

The air smelled of fresh rain, but it was perceptible by feel as well; a heaviness put pressure on the muscles and sinuses.   Jungle sounds chattered in abundance.   This way— a conversation of twittering birds.   That way—a panther's roar receiving a return growl.   From high above fell the laughter of primates.   And in surround sound, leaves rustled, disturbed by creatures that slithered, crawled, and skittered in the shadows.

Gavin stepped forward to be swallowed up by this animated jungle.

It seemed not long enough to hold one's breath before he appeared on the other end, emerging from a curtain of greenery onto a sandy stretch of beachfront.   The bluest crystal ocean greeted him mere strides away, but Gavin's focus wasn't on the clear waters.   It was lifted, peering into a black sky full of twinkling lights.

Stars—or rather, diamonds.

He squinted in the darkness to be sure of his sight.   A frown indented each corner of his mouth when he felt certain his assumption was correct.   Pirates were sailing overhead, flying a black flag with skull and crossbones.   The thieves were en route to steal the stars and pilfer a fortune in diamonds.

"Bly me!" he grumbled to himself.

His dark eyes lowered, glancing over ocean waters. Another ship floated not too far distant in the bay.   Gavin walked across the short stretch of beachfront and waded knee-high into warm waters.   His arms rose in the moonlight, waving back and forth as he cried aloud, hoping to hail the ship.   Miraculously, his ruckus gained someone's attention and a rowboat was sent for him.   Two unshaven scalawags manned the oars, both with a great many missing teeth.   They wore tri-corner caps as shabby as their matching rags. Reaching the young key keeper, they helped him into their boat and then rowed back to a triple-mast sailing ship designated *The Witchery*.

Gavin was greeted aboard by a Captain Jimbo Harvey, one of the fiercest pirates known to unlawfully regulate affairs on Dreamland waters.   A stubborn old rogue, he refused to acknowledge Dreamland as a free nation and claimed the entire area under his rule, calling it 'the scum of Ankergnat' to suit his brigand taste.

A crooked smile glinted of gold behind his coarse whiskers.   His face was masked by a thick, graying beard. His build was medium stock though rock-solid.   On his head sat the widest brim of any hat ever made, and on his shoulder was perched a lime-green parrot.   This bird possessed the ability to command the crew nearly as well as Captain Harvey himself.

"Ahoy thar, Matey.   And what sorta hornswagglin' ideas might ye be havin' in the middle o' the night?   I'll ne'er believe ye be up to much else but dev'lish mischief."

"Then you believe wrong, sir," Gavin informed the captain, "because I'm here to put a stop to the devilish mischief of others currently underway."

Narrowing his gaze suspiciously, the captain asked, "And who's mischief be ye aimin' on interferein' with?"

"That of dishonorable pirates!"

The green parrot raised its feathers and squawked.

Jimbo Harvey backed up, cautious and wary.   His fingers curled around the hilt of a sword fastened to a thick belt that secured his britches.   "Ye be a dern fool then, lad.   A daft sprog to think o' challengin' me surrounded by me own men.   We be nuthin' but honorable gents here, content to lay low o' Jack mischief."

There was a hushed murmur of agreement to their innocence, tainted by a few wicked chuckles.   Gavin realized he'd been misunderstood.

"Oh, no, no, no, I'm not talking about you, Captain Harvey.   The shameful pirates I'm referring to are the ones currently plundering the stars above your heads."

Gavin's pointing finger rose straight up, along with every eye on the ship.   Lo and behold they found the key keeper to be right!   A pirate ship was indeed sailing through black clouds, netting and collecting twinkling diamonds right out of the night.

"Shiver me timbers!   Those scurvy dogs be pluckin' jewels from me rooftop!   How'd them thar villains get by with ne'er a notice?"   The captain scanned his crew for a man who'd look him square in the eye.   No one dared to meet his critical gaze.

He flailed his arms, frustrated, while the parrot on his shoulder copied the gesture with flitting wings.

"Raise them sheets to the wind!   Arm yer stations and prepare for a hearty swashbucklin'!   We've a rival Jolly Roger in our midst!   I swear on the grave of me dear ol' mum we be sinkin' that swaggy and sendin' every last lily-livered crook to an eternal rest in Davy Jones' locker!   Tally ho wi' a vengeance!"

"Aye!   Arrrg!" the men shouted, riled by their captain's speech.

The deck swayed as *The Witchery*'s forward lifted, bowsprit pointing skyward.   All sails roped to masts filled with air and expanded.   The rudder was last to leave the sea. They climbed into the sky on a straight course for rival pirates who remained unaware of their nearing, too busy netting and collecting sparkling jewels.

The Witchery fell silent.   Every grimy member of the crew waited, keen and anxious, as they drifted closer to the vessel Captain Harvey planned to sink.

Gavin patted his thighs.   Out of thin air, matching swords in sheaths appeared at his sides.   He clutched either hilt, ready.

It was the rival pirates who broke the tranquility of the night.

They sounded the alarm, and immediately Captain Harvey gave the order to fire canons.   The enemy ship was shot full of holes but remained hovering above the clouds. Again came an order to fire a second round.   Additional ruptures opened up the bottom decks of the targeted pirate ship. By this time it was on its way around to face off with *The Witchery*.   Gavin glanced at the name painted in black, fancy lettering across the stern of the damaged vessel.   It read *The Red Dagger*.

He gasped.   This was a nightmare ship!   A cursed, unsinkable, haunted craft!   A legend Gavin had heard mention of in many captivating bedtime stories featuring the notorious pirate of greater cunning and fiercer prowess and superior swordsmanship than any other infamous buccaneer!   The captain of this nefarious ship was none other than.......the charcoal-haired Drake Blackmont!

Gavin drew both swords and steadied himself.   This would be a worthy fight for the key keeper—a challenge he truly longed for—if fate paired him off with the most aggressive swordsman ever spoken of in pirate lore.

"Aye."   He licked his lips and grinned at the thought.

There was a blur of motion on either vessel as deckhands rushed to and fro responding to captain's battle orders. Canons fired repeatedly from *The Witchery*, and yet *The Red Dagger* pulled up alongside its attacker, communicating a suicidal wish, daring the enemy to gut its belly hollow. All eyes turned upward, men ducking and cowering from instinct when it rained on Captain Harvey's men. Captain Blackmont had ordered an ambush.

Drake's crew swung from high ropes, falling on *The Witchery* and those sorry souls aboard. Their faces were painted red and black, marked like demons. One glance proved petrifying, causing even the bravest warrior to hesitate. Many of Jimbo's men were run through, paralyzed by initial shock before managing to lift their own swords. But a war cry hit the air and rallied their resolve.

A rabble sword fight engulfed the only ship not ablaze.

Gavin swung his dual blades right and left, exchanging blows using both hands equally well. Every painted figure that came his way met the same fate—cast aside in a motionless heap upon the bloody deck. He fought his way through the crowd, cutting down the enemy, exerting his force with precise, effective moves. But his eye kept focused on the ultimate prize......the captain of *The Red Dagger*.

Drake Blackmont fought on the raised stern, defending his heightened pedestal with a rapier in hand and a case of bold, grinning arrogance.

Gavin paused when he found it his turn to contend with the notorious pirate. He stole a moment to gaze in awe at a legend come to life. Drake paused likewise, swelling with pride at the look of obvious admiration from another soon-to-be victim of his unerring blade.

Gavin raised an eyebrow.   Drake raised one also.

"Aye, lad, yer a young one.   If survival be yer wish today, turn tail now and run.   Run away, and I shan't be forced to cut you down in yer youth."

Setting one foot behind for balance, Gavin gripped tight to his weapons and declared courageously, "I will not run from you."

The legendary captain crooked his head.   "Then yer a fool.   An ignorant, misfortunate fool.   For I am invincible, laddy.   I've walked through fire, carved my way from the guts of dragons, sunk every ship rash enough to give me battle, destroyed whole armies, and cut down countless warriors who believed falsely that a mob had the power to crush me.   I've no fear of death, lad.   Though time and time again he tries, the Grimm Reaper cannot grasp me.   Death is cursed for my sake, ne'er to have my soul.   And so, I've no fear of anything."

"You don't have to be afraid to be defeated, Captain Blackmont."

"Aye, is that right, laddy?"   A pirate smirk conveyed acceptance to a duel.   "Then we shall test yer theory."

As if generously evening the odds, Drake Blackmont placed one hand behind his back.   He jumped down from the heightened deck and met Gavin on level ground.   The two circled once, weapons pointed and ready, eyes glued on one another.   The captain advanced first.   His moves were swifter than anticipated, but Gavin managed to cross his swords and parry the drive downward between his feet.   His pulse pounded in his ears, thumping like deep, base drums.

Thank goodness for quick reflexes.

Captain Blackmont grinned and struck again, whizzing his blade a fraction of an inch past the boy's ear.   Had he wanted it, Drake could've held a severed ear in the palm of his hand.   Gavin retreated quickly, unnerved by his awareness of what could have—*should* have—happened.   His rival gave him no time to consider his luck, but advanced in succession, aiming high, then low, playing with his young challenger. The expert swordsman punctured a shoulder, then a knee, and finally pierced an ear.   Every prick bled droplets of red.

Winded and overwhelmed, Gavin distanced himself from such malicious toying.   His opponent allowed him a moment's rest.

"I gave you a chance to run," Drake smirked darkly. "You should've skedaddled."

Gavin straightened his posture and tossed one sword aside, holding the other before him like a shield.   Perhaps concentrating on a single weapon would prove a better strategy.   He drew air in and out, working to steady his breathing.   Managing a forced smile, he taunted, "I'm just getting started.   I didn't want to hurt your feelings right off, old man."

The captain laughed aloud, amused by the boy's boldness.   Though minor scuffles continued to take place around them, the two had drawn a crowd.   Only Drake seemed aware of the fact.

He attacked without a hint of warning—a thrust aimed at a thigh.   Gavin parried the blow, scuttling backwards to avoid a strike.   As Drake recovered, he easily deflected a desperate jab meant for his heart.   Then the captain lunged forward again, swift as metallic lightning.   Gavin parried, retreating.   It was nothing but a dance for Captain Blackmont and an exercise in self-defense for the boy.

After barely holding off a sequence of fancy brandishing, Gavin found himself on his back looking up at the pointed end of a rapier.   He'd tripped over a coil of rope while avoiding his opponent's blade.   It had happened faster than his mind could register.

"Avast! Leave the boy be!" It was Captain Harvey running to his aide, but there was no need for anyone's interference.

Beneath Gavin's shirt an amber glow sparked, growing bright enough to catch the attention of onlookers. Its radiance reached into the darkness.

"It's my key," Gavin said. "I have to go; someone's near the gates."

Drake withdrew his sword and slipped it into the sheath at his side. "Aye! Get along, key keeper. I'm sure we'll meet up again."

Gavin jumped to his feet. And so did every other character on board who'd been lying motionless as if struck dead by a rival sword. *The Red Dagger* was no longer ablaze, but appeared whole and solid as if it had never suffered one blast from a canon.

Strange? Not really. For that is another secret Gavin keeps. Aye, ya see, me hearties, in Dreamland all lads and lasses and e'en sly ol' buccaneers ne'er, e'er taste the sting o' death. In proper words…

No one ever really dies in Dreamland.

Chapter Three
Brotherly Love

It was turning into a busy night for the young key keeper. He'd been summoned once again to lure away dreamers who'd ventured too near the gates of his home. This sort of occurrence was normally rare. If the never-ending hall of doors didn't tempt a trespasser to the wayside, the guardians usually frightened them off. Few managed to reach the outskirts of Dreamland without confronting the guardians.

The guardians? Oh dear, did I forget to mention them? No, no, I believe they were spoken of previously, but I'll admit I may have failed to call the beasts by their true title.

The guardians are in fact those hideous monsters concealed within the shadows of Dreamland's surrounding forest. They are terrifying creatures—the essence of a spine-chilling nightmare! With giant eyes like a pair of full moons bulging from fur-covered faces, and fangs as sharp as daggers snapping over a nasty growl, and claws protracting from heavy paws, these ferocious monsters perform their function well; they act as deterrents to anyone nearing the ivy-covered gates.

But as horrific as these guardians happen to be, they do sometimes fail in their purpose. This was the present case.

Gavin snuck up behind a foursome of boys crouched side by side by side behind a screen of high underbrush.

"What are we staring at?" the key keeper asked softly.

The boys were so focused on the object of their spying, this whisper caused them to jump and scurry from a perceived threat. In his alarmed retreat, the oldest boy stammered a warning. He was the tallest of the boys, anyway—near Gavin's height— making him appear to be the eldest.

"S..s..stay away! I..I..I mean it; you stay away or..or..or *else!*"

The others gaped at the stranger, all of them sharing the same big blue eyes. By the same token, each wore a red mop top and pale skin speckled with freckles. It was obvious they were siblings.

Gavin smiled and replied coolly, "These are my woods. I live nearby here." His calm manner seemed to relax the boys, but only by a degree.

"What's your name?" the eldest asked.

"Gavin. What's yours?"

"Daniel. These are my brothers—Delbert, Dillan, and Donovan."

The key keeper kept himself from laughing, though his lips twitched with amusement. How silly for all their names to begin with the same letter.

"What are you doing in my woods?   Who were you spying on?"

Daniel shifted on his feet, appearing sorry for being caught trespassing on someone's property.   "Did you know your woods are infested with wild monsters?"

The key keeper lifted an eyebrow, not in answer but as a sign for the boy to continue talking.

"We have another brother.   He's just a baby—only four years old."

"Let me guess," Gavin cut in.   "His name is….Davis?"

"No.   His name is Douglas—or Duggie, as Mum likes to call him."

The key keeper hid a snickering grin.

"We were minding our own business, following a trail that steered us through your trees, when we were attacked by a pack of hairy beasts.   We tried to run from them, but Doug was snatched up and taken!   So we've been spying on the terrible creatures hoping to get a glimpse of our brother."

Gavin's brow pulled low and taut.   That didn't sound like something the guardians would do.   Perhaps the boy was mistaken.

The smallest and gangliest of the brothers, the one named Donovan, spoke up timidly with his opinion.   His expression communicated serious concern.   "I think Duggie might've been eaten."

Gavin screwed up his face.   "And why in the world would you think that?"

The boy held up a small pair of red sneakers. "Because we found his shoes without him in 'em."

Gavin glanced at the shoes and then twisted his neck in the opposite direction.   Squinting, he peered out into the woods.   The guardians accused of swallowing the youngest

'D' brother were nowhere to be seen.

"I'm sure the beasts haven't eaten him," the key keeper announced with confidence. "They have no appetite for baby food."

But Daniel didn't appear convinced, nor did his siblings. They were clearly anxious about the matter.

"Then where is our brother?" Dillan asked.

"Yeah," seconded Delbert. "What have those monsters done with Duggie?"

"Why would they take him?" Donovan worried. "Is he…..is he in danger?"

Four freckled faces stared at Gavin, expecting answers. The key keeper responded by moving into the trees, rounding his arm as a signal for everyone to come along.

"I'll find him for you."

The inexperienced hunting party trudged through the forest in a line. There was no trodden path to follow. Out of necessity, their knees lifted high with each and every step that pushed them through heavy underbrush. The four brothers trailed a complete stranger without hesitation, accepting him as a self-proclaimed expert in the ways of monsters.

After half a mile of quiet hiking, the oldest boy seemed ready to question their rash placement of trust. He asked about the lack of monstrous paw prints in their path. That's when Gavin halted, shushing everyone with a finger pressed to his lips. He motioned for them to squat low and keep hidden. All eyes flashed ahead, necks straining to search for the reason why.

Not far beyond a screen of tree trunks, five hairy guardians with sharp fangs and horns were gathered in a small clearing. A noise resembling deep, guttural growls purred from the pack. With a little imagination, it was an easy stretch to interpret the low rumble as beastly laughter.

34

Daniel inched closer to crouch beside Gavin for a better look. He spoke in whispers. "I don't see Doug anywhere. Where is he? What have they done with him?"

The moment those fretful questions crossed his lips, a squeal that could only be taken as a toddler's giggle rang through the air. Daniel and his brothers gasped at the sight of four-year-old Duggie flying in a high arch across the open circle. But his body didn't fall to the ground. It came to a jerky stop midair and then whipped right back. The little boy laughed delightedly at the tickle in his tummy from being thrashed about.

"Oh no!" Daniel exclaimed. He stood up as if he would confront the throng of monsters, but Gavin pulled him back down by the arm.

"Wait, wait a minute. Your brother's fine. Look."

Daniel—along with Delbert, Dillan, and Donovan who'd made their way up to stand shoulder to shoulder with the big boys—squinted to see things more clearly. Their littlest brother was still zipping here and there through the air, giggling gleefully. But careful observation showed him grasping onto an unclear detail—something thin and long and loppy tossing him about. An even closer look revealed Douglas had an unshakable hold on a monster's tail. The creature attached to the other end didn't appear the slightest bit happy about it.

Gavin chuckled at a sudden comprehension of events and proceeded to explain his amusement to four boys wearing knitted brows. "Your brother's got a monster by the tail, lucky devil! And by the looks of things, he's not about to let go."

"I noticed that," Daniel grumbled. He still didn't see an ounce of humor in the situation.

"Don't you know what it means to catch a monster by

the tail?"

The 'D' brothers exchanged clueless glances.

Gavin chuckled again. "Why it means he becomes your pet! Your bond beast! He's yours to order around! That is until you let go of his tail."

Daniel glanced out at the monsters again. "Is that why he's being flung around? Is the monster trying to shake him off?"

"I don't think so," Gavin said. "It looks to me like your baby brother is having his own kind of fun."

Every eye returned to the bizarre scene. The wiggly tail seemed to lose its liveliness when it dropped abruptly, thumping Duggie on his hind end in the soft grass. The little boy cricked his neck to look up into the grim features of a huge, hairy face that for anyone else would've provoked terror. But the toddler simply smiled wide and exclaimed, "Again, again! Me go again!"

At that childish wish, the monster groaned in gravely protest, but it lifted its tail nonetheless, whipping it back and forth and back another time to appease his young master. Duggie held on, laughing giddily.

Those watching in the shadows laughed too—brief, hesitant chuckles—as they understood their brother was not in harm's way as assumed.

Daniel leaned in to whisper in Gavin's ear. "How can I get Doug away from those monsters without them turning to attack us? I don't want my brothers to get hurt."

The key keeper cocked his head sideways. He made a face at Daniel, scrunching his nose and curling his upper lip.

"I'm serious," the eldest brother insisted, feeling as if he'd ignorantly asked a stupid question.

"You don't know anything about monsters, do you?"

The young man shrugged and scratched his head.

"Well, um…….no."

Gavin turned himself to face Daniel full on, prepared to share a big and valuable secret.

"A monster's worst fear is of being found.   They never attack people."

He went on with an explanation for the confused young man.   "Monsters growl and roar and screech and howl and stomp their feet and lash their tails and swipe their claws, but it's all an act.   They're far too afraid to attack; they just want to frighten you away.   Now a gargoyle, an ogre, a goblin, a troll, or a dragon might tear after you, but not those hairy beasts out there.   Those wild fur-balls are simple shadow monsters.   And the reason they lurk in their own shadows is because they're afraid of yours."

"You mean to say…."   There was a contemplative pause.   "You're telling me those scary-looking beasts are *afraid of us?*"

"Yes, Daniel.   Why else would they hide in closets and beneath staircases and under beds?   They're hoping you'll never find them because all they really want is to be left alone."

"Then why did those monsters jump out of the trees and growl at us earlier?   We were minding our own business."

"You'd crossed into their territory; they were trying to scare you off.   That's all they wanted was for you to turn tail and run."

"And believe me, that's exactly what we did!   Until we realized Doug was missing."

"Your baby brother somehow managed to grab onto a monster's tail during all the fuss."   Gavin laughed at the mental picture.   "And now he's using the poor beast to have his fun! He doesn't even realize the power he has gripped in his hands!"

"I'm just glad he's okay," Daniel sighed, a sheer sound of relief. "But again, I'm asking you, how do we get him away from those creatures?"

"Don't worry. I've got an idea."

The key keeper remained in a low squat as he waddled like a duck through the underbrush. His eyes were focused on the ground, searching, while his hands parted grass and leaves to reveal things hidden within. He ignored all slithering, crawling life forms in favor of one that hopped. Cupping both hands, he scooped up a slimy, green frog.

The 'D' brothers watched. A mask of confusion twisted up every one of their freckled faces.

Gavin merely grinned beneath a quick wink and then waddled off, shuffling low in the grass, closer and closer to the pet beast Duggie ignorantly kept in his hold. Gavin stopped at the final tree before the clearing, using its broad trunk as a hiding place. He brought his cupped hands up to one eye and peeked through a tiny gap between his fingers, checking on the frog trapped inside. Sucking in enough air to completely fill up his lungs and both cheeks, the key keeper held his breath. Then he brought his hands to his lips and exhaled into the hole between his thumb and forefinger.

Daniel, Dillan, Delbert, and Donovan watched closely. They took on even greater looks of confusion before every freckled boy dropped his mouth wide open.

Gavin's hands were forced apart as the frog in his clutches swelled to seven times its original size. The head portion—especially the frog's chin—stretched sheer as it filled with air. The result was a green balloon.

A frog balloon.

The novelty behaved like it would float away, but

38

Gavin held onto one long, skinny leg. Leaning out from his hiding place, he silently shoved the bloated frog in the direction of the monsters, aiming it downward toward the giggling five-year-old.

Duggie noticed it right off. The balloon drifted slowly closer and closer, two beady eyes blinking at the very top. It rose by inches as it traveled. Duggie squealed with delight and reached, but the frog balloon evaded him.

"Up, up!" he pointed, wanting his furry playmate to lift him within reach of this new toy. But the little boy had made a critical error. He'd released the monster's tail in order to point all ten fingers at the rising balloon. The shadow monster now turned on him, along with the rest of the pack.

They growled and hissed and roared with thunderous voices. Towering above the child like hungry grizzlies over a cowering rabbit, they did what monsters do best.

They scared the pants off the brat.

Duggie screamed and wailed. Tears pooled in his eyes as he took to his hands and knees, moving into the fastest crawl he could manage. At that very moment his brothers jumped out from the surrounding trees.

Daniel raised his arms and pretended to claw at the air, forcing a wild roar to rise from deep down in his gut.

Dillan and Delbert flailed their arms about and jumped up and down while howling and cawing in the most annoying of high pitches.

Donovan ran to Duggie's aid, picking him up and hugging him tight.

It seemed like a standoff for the longest minute in their young lives—a lofty line of monsters snarling ferociously at a minor line of screeching, bug-eyed boys—until Gavin stepped in and urged them all to run.

"Follow me! Come quickly and follow me!"

They didn't need persuading.

The boys ran and ran, dodging trees and low-lying branches. Though many times their eyes turned backwards, no one glimpsed a single monster. Daniel was the first to slow.

"I think we've lost 'em," he breathed, winded. "We're safe now."

His brothers nodded in agreement. All but Duggie panted to catch a decent breath. The baby was still crying, reaching skyward. Donvan set his brother down carefully, but Duggie stomped his tiny feet until he stumbled and fell backwards onto his rump. This made him cry even harder.

"He's just shook up," Donovan guessed, kneeling beside his wailing brother to administer a few comforting pats on the back.

"No, that's not it," Daniel surmised after a moment of observation. "He's reaching for that balloon. He wants that silly frog balloon." Daniel turned to Gavin. "How did you do that anyway?"

The key keeper grinned. "Why, it's as easy as breathing in and out."

The 'D' brothers waited for an explanation, except for Duggie who continued to bawl persistently.

Gavin paused to frown down on the boy. "He's kind of spoiled, isn't he?"

Dillan and Delbert rolled their eyes while Daniel groaned, "You've no idea."

Ignoring the child's tantrum, Gavin brought both hands to rest on his hips. His back arched the slightest bit as he used his stomach muscles to form a croak. The sound was pushed from deep down, clear up his throat, and out.

"Gribbit! Gribbit! Gribbit!"

In no time at all an army of frogs leapt from the

surrounding shrubbery, attracted by the key keeper's call. Little, green, slimy amphibians gathered in the grass everywhere. Their beady eyes stared up at Gavin while their chins expanded and deflated with each croak.

"Way cool!" Dillan breathed.

"Yeah, super neat!" Delbert agreed.

Even their baby brother seemed impressed, stopping his tantrum long enough to glance over the crowd of green hoppers. The distraction lasted for only a moment. Donovan patted his brother's back when Duggie burst into sobs once again.

"Grab a frog," Gavin instructed.

His onlookers did as they were told. As soon as every boy had one of the slippery critters hidden within his cupped hands—all but crybaby Douglas, that is—the key keeper continued.

"Now, make a little opening....like this." Gavin showed how bending his thumb created a gap between his fingers. "You'll feel your frog put his lips up to the hole. They always do that. Take a peek and see."

The boys brought their balled-up hands to their eyes.

"Whoa!"

"Neat!"

"Way cool!"

"Okay, now what?"

"Now suck in a deep breath, the deeper the better, and hold it." Everyone copied the instructor as he performed the action.

In a tight voice that attempted not to use up the air trapped in his lungs, Gavin squeaked, "Kiss the frog's mouth and blow." He was about to demonstrate when a chorus of objections stopped him.

"Yuck!"

"Gross!"

"I'm not gonna kiss a slimy frog!"

"Are you serious?"

Gavin scanned a line of disgusted expressions. He frowned. "What's the matter? Are you afraid of catching a case of frog warts?"

Dillan and Delbert exchanged wary glances. "Is that possible?"

"No!" The key keeper huffed through his nose in frustration. "If you want to act like a girl, fine; although, girls at least have a good excuse for not kissing frogs."

Daniel appeared to wonder what that could be. Gavin volunteered the answer. "When a girl kisses a frog there's always a chance he might turn into a lousy prince. It can be real upsetting when that happens."

Ignoring their shock and reservations, Gavin drew in another lungful of air and puckered his lips. He pressed them to the small opening in his hands and kissed the slimy lips sticking out. Then he blew. The frog's head expanded, ballooned by Gavin's exhale. Smiling proudly, he offered the swollen frog to crybaby Duggie, handing it over by a skinny frog leg.

The four-year-old beamed, ceasing his tears more quickly than a sunrise lights up the sky. He giggled and grabbed the balloon. He waved it in the air. He clapped his hands and——let go. Young Douglas watched the balloon float out of reach. Making a sour face, the baby began to wail.

His brothers overcame their reservations instantly. Within the time it took to breathe in and out, they were holding four more ballooned frogs in his face. Duggie laughed and clapped and swatted at the offered toys. He rose to his feet and jumped up and down, grabbing for the balloons and then letting them go to float up, up, up past the treetops.   He set the poor frogs free nearly as quickly as his brothers could inflate fresh ones.

Daniel paused long enough to thank their new friend. "I really do appreciate your help rescuing Doug."

"No big deal," Gavin shrugged.

"Well, it is to me.   I was honestly worried those hairy monsters would have him for dinner.   I wasn't sure what I was going to tell Mum."

The key keeper saw a perfect opportunity, and he took it.

"If you want my advice, from here on out I'd steer clear of dark forests.   There's almost always a pack of monsters hiding somewhere in the shadows.   And none of them are friendly to trespassers."

Daniel nodded.   "I think I'll heed your advice."

While the eldest boy visited, and the three middle boys gathered a new supply of frogs, young Douglas stole a moment to wander off unobserved.   He'd spotted something unusual sitting in the trees which tore his attention away from the many floating frog balloons.   It was a brown, solid piece of wood propped up lengthwise.   When he reached it, he recognized a pleasant humming coming from the other side.

"Mummy!   Mummy!" he exclaimed.

His small fingers stretched to turn at a knob just barely within his reach by tiptoe.   With effort, he twisted it just enough to crack the door open.   Daniel glanced up in time to see his baby brother step over the threshold and disappear.

"Doug!"   Looking wildly at the key keeper, Daniel begged an explanation.

Gavin offered one, urging every brother to hearken. "Duggie's fine.   He simply found the way home.   Go on, you can follow him.   Your mother is waiting for you through that doorway."

With perfect, youthful faith they obeyed.   Daniel was the last to vanish.

Gavin's lips spread thin, grinning from ear to ear.   He had proved successful in guarding Dreamland's gates once again.   For the fun of it, he kissed another frog and ballooned the little critter, sending him adrift in a cool breeze.   The light of sunrise shone through a gap in the treetops, enhancing the colors of the leaves.

"Hmmm," he hummed, staring up.   "I didn't realize it was so early.   I better head for home myself."

Chapter Four
The Trouble with Parents

In Dreamland, like any other world, people are divided into families. And, like in any other world, there are differences of opinion and clashing personalities that cause struggles in the home. It's unavoidable. Parents and children naturally tug on opposite ends of a power rope. They disagree on choices while fighting for autonomy. For the noble key keeper living with his mother and father, the same challenges existed. And so you will see…

Inside the glittering white gates of Dreamland, Gavin

rushed in the direction of home, determined to beat a rising sun to the front door. He managed to reach his front steps only seconds before sunlight painted the cement white from gray. He paused for a moment to watch the sky bleach—a pale blue almost as white as the clouds. Grinning like a rascally goblin, he imagined the sun glaring as hot and red as an ember. Then he pictured the sky bleeding vibrant orange. The colors spread overhead at his wishes, warming everything above the horizon and dulling the jungle bordering his home.

To alter the sky or the landscape is no unusual happening in this wondrous world. How is that, you ask? Don't tell me you've already forgotten the greatest secret of Dreamland! The one that must be guarded and kept at all costs? The one that grants any person a touch of wizard's magic? Yes, yes, that's the one!

Reality in Dreamland is whatever you want it to be.

This means the sky might appear orange for Gavin and blue for his father and as yellow as a dandelion for his mother. Their house may sit in a rain forest or on a deserted island or within an affluent neighborhood all at the same time because each person sees the world in his or her own way. Strange? No, not really. Even outside of Dreamland, reality depends a great deal upon one believing what he sees—or seeing what he believes. Either way.

Stepping through the front door, Gavin announced himself. "Mother! Father! I'm home!"

Rounding a wall at the end of the foyer, he found his parents sitting down to breakfast in a clean and cozy kitchen. A tall, slender woman dressed in flowing skirts stood up from a lace-covered table and smiled at her son. Her dark eyes glinted with admiration. Brown lengths of hair appeared to

46

undulate in the light, the long waves falling forward as she leaned down to place a third plate of food on the table.

"Come and eat, Gavin. We have a number of important things to attend to today, and we *will not* be late to parliament."

Gavin moved to take the cushioned seat pulled out for him, avoiding his mother's stern eye. She was a loving and devoted woman but not a character to oppose. Not without good reason, anyway.

"Of course, Mother. We'll be on time."

"Yes, we will. And I would like to see you change your clothes before then."

He glanced at his black pants and shirt. A black belt hugged his waste, adorned by a silver buckle decorated with the likeness of a roaring beast.

"What's wrong with my clothes? They're not soiled."

His mother made a face that creased her pointy nose. "The pants are fine, I suppose, but I would prefer a nicer shirt. Something stunning and fashionable and…...and not black."

Unhappy with the idea but knowing better than to refuse his mother, Gavin imagined himself in a collared, gold shirt with long sleeves draping his arms. Crisscrossed laces tied up the front. It was simple in design, yet elegant in both feel and color. A compromise.

"I suppose that's better," his mother sighed after his clothing magically transformed. She was being generous by meeting him halfway.

Gavin looked down at the breakfast prepared for him. It was a nutritious mix of dried fruits and heated grains. A glass of milk was set beside his plate. The young man glanced at the head of the table to where his father, finely dressed, sat reading the latest copy of '*The Dreamland Chronicle*'.

The man was a spitting image of his son but with shorter curls and sharper angles to his round features. He sipped on a hot cup of dried, ground, organic root that had been seeped in scalding water. The vapors carried an earthy scent, bringing to mind images of roasted tree bark. Gavin groaned internally, pitying how his father stooped to such insufferable depths to please his wife. The boy had no intention of ever finding himself bewitched by a girl in that way. To imagine voluntarily forcing oneself to sip cup after nasty cup of wretched, percolated blekcack root just to keep a pampered woman happy.......*yech!*

His eyes fell back on his own plate of health food. A simple wish improved the menu under his nose, transforming his breakfast into a dessert tray—candy truffles, cream puffs, and warm bubbleberry muffins! From the corner of his eye Gavin caught his father's raised brow. His mother took a seat across the table, pausing with her steaming mug of blekcack root to sigh disapprovingly at her son's choice of foods.

"Gavin, really!" she groaned. "We are scheduled to stand before parliament in less than an hour where we will be surrounded by the grandest of company. You are to report in full public view today."

Gavin shrugged the morning's events off as no big deal. He was often before parliament reporting on his duties as key keeper.

His mother's eyebrows lifted as high as they could rise. "And do you know what bubbleberries do to a person?"

Squirming a bit, Gavin answered truthfully. "Well, they um.....they form bubbles in your stomach."

"And...?" his mother pressed, expectant in her expression.

"And uh.....sometimes.....the bubbles rise up your throat."

"—or your nose," his father added. His grin vanished at one look from his wife who promptly returned to the task of questioning her son.

"And what else escapes your throat?"

"Ohhh.....a noise?"

Her patience was shot. "Gavin! Bubbleberries make a person *burp out loud!* I really don't need you embarrassing our family by burping up bubbles in front of parliament today!"

"Alright, Mother, alright." Gavin exchanged brief humored glances with his father before wishing the berry muffins off his plate. He dove right into a cream puff, taking a big bite out of the crust.

His mother blinked her long lashes over rolling eyes. "Would it really hurt you to keep a healthier diet?"

"Yes," he muttered with a mouthful of whipped cream.

The man of the house sat up straight in his chair and chose that moment to exert his authority. The tone he used put an end to further bickering at the table.

"Gavin, mind your manners and add a pear to your plate." His eyes turned a degree softer on his wife. "Sweetheart, the boy is in no danger of malnutrition. Let it go."

The proud woman brought her mug to her lips and fell moodily quiet for as long as it took to sip half the drink down. Then she changed the subject with another question.

"So.......what sort of adventures did you have last night, Gavin?"

He grinned and swallowed a mouthful of chocolate. "You'll never guess who I dueled with!"

His father's interest was roused. The newspaper hiding his face folded over before being lowered to the table. He made repeated stabs at the answer.

"Lancelot del Lac of the round table."

"No, sir."

"King Arthur of Camelot himself!"

"No, sir.

"Athos or Porthos or...what was his name? You know, the third musketeer?"

"No, Father, none of them. Think more along the lines of famed villains."

"Of course," his mother grumbled, sipping at her blekcack.

"Oooooh. Okay, okay.........Ali Baba...no, no....Aaron the Moor...no, no, no.... *Long John Silver!*"

"No, sir, but you're getting warmer."

"Hmmmm. A pirate then?"

Gavin nodded, unable to keep from grinning."

"Captain Harvey?"

"Not quite."

Gavin's father looked to the ceiling as he concentrated on a mental list of notorious pirates. His dark eyes glinted when he realized the obvious answer. "*Ah-hah*, of course! Drake Blackmont! Unparalleled swordsman and captain of the Red Dagger!"

Gavin's smile stretched from ear to ear. "Yes, sir!"

His father leaned back in his chair. "So—how long did it take him to run you through?"

A female gasp hit the air.

"He didn't actually run me through. I was summoned to the gates before the duel ended, but I was flat on my back staring up at the tip of his sword at the time. I think I managed a good five minutes before he took me down."

"Not bad, not bad. Maybe next time you'll stretch it out to six before he spears you."

The lady of the house exhaled with a shudder. "And what makes you think my son won't beat that cruel-and-nasty

Captain Blackmont next time?"

Two wide-eyed stares turned her way, looking horrified by her naïve suggestion.   They quickly explained the taboos of tampering with established Dreamland tradition.

"No one *ever* beats Drake Blackmont in a duel, Mother. Not e*ver!*"

A sound of refusal escaped her throat.   "Well of course you can beat him, anyone can.   Just imagine yourself victor and run him through.   *Ta-dah!*   You win!"

Gavin grabbed his stomach as if he would be sick.

His father put a hand to his forehead and groaned. "Ohhh, Sweetheart.   Love.   There are lines we do not cross. And *this......this tradition* is an *imperative* line.   Captain Drake Blackmont has always proved victor in each and every battle he's ever faced since.....well, since the beginning of time!   Have you any idea how many people you would anger by simply wishing yourself winner in a duel with such an esteemed master swordsman?"

"He's nothing but a nasty pirate."

Gavin gaped.   His father cringed.

"He's a hero, Mother—an icon!   He's every boy's champion!"

"Sweetheart.   Darling.   Captain Blackmont is the lion all men strive to be but fall short of—no exceptions!"

Two against one, the lady of the house realized there'd be no talking sense into the pair.   "Fine," she sighed in concession.   "Be daft enough to let yourselves get run through then."

Father and son answered in loyal harmony.   "We will!"

Breakfast ended abruptly and the three prepared to head out.

In the very heart of the city, Dreamland's parliament meets daily to conduct governing affairs. This elected group consists of twenty and seven judicious, white-haired men and women whom Gavin likes to refer to as '*The Wizened Society*'. This because of their mutual elderly appearance. The capitol building in which they meet is a magnificent structure similar to a cathedral, having spires and stained glass windows and artistic craftwork embellishing every inch of trim inside and out. Gavin often imagines gruesome stone gargoyles sitting atop the roof, holding tight to each and every spire. He pictures them waiting for him to exit the building before magically transforming into living, snarling man-hunters. For Gavin, battling any monstrous creature or villain is pure fun.

The highest heads of parliament—seven honored members of the main body—often call on the key keeper to appear before them. They hear his reports on activities outside the city gates and then pass along important news to the whole of parliament. This day, however, all twenty and seven members were present to discuss concerns about the increasing number of dreamers wandering too near the outer walls.

When asked to approach the podium, Gavin stood up tall, taking confident steps toward the stand. His pointed chin lifted proudly as he faced a half-circle of delegates. His father and mother remained in their seats, watching and beaming. A pudgy man resembling a hobbit stood at an opposite podium and read off a number of related questions.

"Key keeper, is it true your key has summoned you to our city's gates more and more frequently in the last four cycles of the Ploris moon? Is it also true that the number of dreamers roaming near our borders has greatly increased? Have the guardians failed repeatedly in deterring unwanted trespassers? And have these circumstances made it necessary for you to employ creative measures to lure dreamers away from our city?"

Gavin answered with a simple 'yes' to all of the above questions.

The interrogator made a grim face. "Then it is as I feared. Dreamland stands in danger of invasion."

There was a mix of gasps and murmurs reacting to such a bold statement. The same reactions came from members of parliament as from concerned citizens witnessing the proceedings.

Gavin spoke over the noise with a loud and assured, "No, your grace, that is not so."

The hobbit-looking gentleman turned back to him, raising a white line of bushy eyebrows.

Gavin went on. "I don't believe there is any threat of invasion from dreamers. While it's true some are finding their way to our gates, the majority never even notice the wall. They wander close simply due to their own curious dreams. I've managed to steer every one of them away without endangering the secrets of our great city."

"But they come, do they not? In greater numbers than ever!"

Gavin avoided a natural tendency to nod, not wanting to reinforce the old man's fears. He asked the dignitary a question of his own, mentioning a group of spirit beings called whisperers. These ghostly whisperers were responsible for patrolling the city in search of gatecrashers. Their task—to confront and chase off any trespasser by means of persuasion.

"Your grace, has there been any need for the whisperers to descend upon an intruder?"

The white-haired gentleman cast a quizzical glance at his colleagues. A few shook their heads. "No, key keeper, the whisperers have not been called upon for many cycles of the Ploris moon."

"And have I, as your key keeper, even once complained about added hardship in my duties?"

There was a consensus of smiles from parliament. "No, young man, you have been reliable and vigilant in your calling."

It was tempting for Gavin to glance over his shoulder and catch a sure sign of pride from his parents, but he resisted, concentrating on the matter at hand.

"However—" the delegate continued, raising a firm finger, "there have been warning signs that mustn't be carelessly overlooked. An unusual few know more than we do about the ambitions of dreamers. If you wouldn't mind stepping down, key keeper, we would like to call one such individual to the stand. Traveler, will you step forward?"

"A traveler?" Gavin wasn't the only stunned individual to breathe the same astonished question.

Travelers, just so you know, are citizens of Dreamland who've chosen not to live within the city's gates. Their numbers are small, and they rarely return to dwell within the borders of Dreamland. They're considered aimless souls— sad and lonely individuals who wander about in some unknown beyond. What actually exists out there is a mystery to most but is popularly considered an empty void. It is space used by dreamers who, when asleep, materialize and act out their bizarre fantasies. Then, when they awaken to their own physical world, these dreamers and their imagined fantasies vanish. Even Gavin, familiar with areas outside Dreamland, never once traveled much of a distance from the city's influence. Rumors suggest the void eventually drops off like the last step on a stairwell, depositing the wayward traveler into a physical realm—a harsh, non-magical reality. But the truth is that few know the truth.

The moment Gavin took his seat beside his mother, she

leaned in to worry in his ear. "Why are they questioning you like this? What have you done?"

He shot her an offended look. "Nothing, Mother!"

She went on, ignoring his reaction. "Your father should've stepped forward and taken the stand. He was highly respected as key keeper before you, and he knows the challenges and difficulties facing the calling."

"It's not a difficult task, Mother. The guardians and the whisperers both assist me."

"It's an important position you hold, Gavin. One not to be taken lightly."

"I know, but it's not a challenge. I'm good at this calling. I enjoy being key keeper."

"I'm not disputing your abilities, son, but to earn parliament's trust…"

He made another sore face. "They *do* trust me!"

This time she acknowledged his bruised feelings, patting his thigh consolingly. "Yes, yes, I'm sure that's true, but…..their faith appears to be wavering. Your father's testimony could help strengthen it."

"Why do you say that?"

"Because…" She hesitated, glancing at the man she spoke of on her other side. "Because he's been beyond the barrier lands. You father has visited the world where so-called dreamers come from."

Gavin's eyes grew big as he leaned past his mother to look at his father. "You've been……out *there?*"

A grave face turned toward the boy. "Yes, son, I have." Clearly the memory was a burden of past sorrows. Gavin's father exhaled solemnly. "That's where I met your mother."

Chapter Five
A Traveler's Tale

Gavin suddenly had a million questions. His head swirled with bewilderment. He asked the obvious.

"You, Mother? You were one of......one of *them?*"

His parents nodded in sync, and his mother quietly admitted the truth. "A dreamer, yes. At one time—ages and ages ago—I was a part of their world."

He gawked at the woman beside him, unable to see her in the same familiar light as a moment ago. Sure, he was aware of those rare occurrences when a sly, skillful, or persistent dreamer had crossed over the gates of Dreamland.

And it was true that few who entered were ever persuaded by the whisperers to leave. But his own mother—an infiltrator?

"How in the world did you get past Father to scale the wall?"

"She didn't," Gavin's father answered. Again, his eyes seemed to frown at a distant memory. He took his wife's hand in his own and admitted, "I lured her inside. She had no idea this place even existed."

Gavin's wide eyes flickered back and forth between his parents who were looking sadly at one another. The boy couldn't think to form another coherent question. But he didn't have to. His father, Dreamland's previous key keeper, offered up an explanation willingly.

"There weren't many dreamers approaching the gates in my day, and those who did usually fled at the sight of a guardian, being innocent enough to fear shadow monsters. But one young woman managed to reach the wall. She was brushing her fingers over the keyhole, tracing its shape, when I approached her. Her eyes were bright with curiosity, her will strongly stubborn. She was determined to find the key that matched the outline in the stone, convinced some magical land existed beyond the wall—a place she was determined to get to. It was easy enough to convince her that a treasure hunt might turn up the key. I presented her with a map, one I'd created out of sheer desperation. It led to no place in particular, but went on for miles and miles away from Dreamland. Eager and grateful, the young lady took it from me. She asked for my assistance searching for the key. Having nothing better to do, I agreed to accompany her. The hunt steered us far from Dreamland—further than I'd ever before ventured."

"Was it Mother you were helping?"

"No, son, it wasn't me. It was my sister."

Gavin's features tangled up in a befuddled manner.

His mother turned to her husband and gestured the slightest bit for him to continue the story.

"Your mother's sister returned many times to the wall, having memorized the pathway to reach it. The guardians and the hall of doors couldn't deter her resolve to find the key she was certain would grant her access. It was amusing to me that she never once thought to try scaling the wall."

"I don't think she knew how to climb," Gavin's mother cut in. "My sister couldn't even walk, except for in her dreams. She was paralyzed from the waist down, the result of a childhood…..mishap."

Again Gavin caught a miserable, furtive glance shared between his parents. There was more they were hiding from him, but to push the issue felt like an invasion of privacy.

"So, where did Mother come in?" the boy asked instead.

Gavin's father went on recounting the past while holding his wife's hand. "I followed the young woman numerous times further and further from Dreamland, telling myself I was being vigilant in my calling by keeping a close eye on a potential threat to our city. But the truth was, I felt as much curiosity about where she disappeared to every day as she felt about what existed beyond the stone wall in her dreams. One day I followed her clear into her world. A physical world for her, but not for me. I existed like a phantom there—unseen by everyone, and unable to grasp or touch anything. All I could do was witness the lives of people so unlike myself."

"How so? Father, tell me, how are they different?"

His parents exchanged a painful look. When his father's eyes dropped, jaw clenched, Gavin worried he was being refused any more information. But his mother took over at that point.

"Not everyone is kind where I'm from, Gavin. Not that everyone is kind here either. Consider your famed pirate, for example. But the difference lies in the fact that being pierced with a sword in Dreamland leaves no lasting consequences. No one really gets hurt. In the world where I was born....well.....you see....."

When she couldn't seem to form the words, her husband did.

"People die, Gavin."

"What do you mean, they die?" This wasn't a concept the young man was familiar with.

His father tried to explain. "The dead are no longer alive, no longer active. They don't breathe or move or play or open their eyes. They just cease to exist."

Gavin's puzzled stare darted between both parents. "Where do they go then?"

"Nowhere."

The idea was incomprehensible. "How can that be? Can't you wish them back?"

"No, dear. You can't wish things into reality where I came from. It's nothing like Dreamland. Something gone is gone forever. And a thing that exists cannot be wished away."

"Unless it dies?"

His father nodded assuredly. "Yes. Unless it…she...dies."

Gavin made a presumption, one he was fairly sure of. "Your sister died?"

His mother turned her head into her shoulder, hiding revisited grief within long strands of hair. Her husband offered comfort in his arms, but she refused him, not wanting to draw further attention to herself in a public setting. Gavin squirmed at the muffled sound of weeping.

"I'm sorry, Mother," he whispered, placing a hand on her arm. "I'm sorry for what I said." He glanced at his father, unsure, begging for assistance.

The man shook his head helplessly in response.

It only took a minute for the weeping woman to compose herself again. She immediately summarized the rest of the story, keeping herself together by tensing every muscle.

"My sister died because she was hurt by someone. I was badly hurt at the same time. Your father witnessed it all, but he was unable to do anything. An illusion can't stop a…"

"I wasn't an illusion."

"You know what I mean. Anyway…...he waited for me to dream and then approached me, offering to take me to Dreamland with him. He made it sound like a wonderful paradise, a world safe from pain and suffering. So I accepted."

"You saved Mother." Gavin met his father's gaze, but the man lowered his head, mumbling what sounded like a near apology.

"That was my intention. I meant no harm. I was trying to protect her the only way I knew how, in the only place my influence could make a difference."

Gavin was confused. By all appearances he *had* protected her—saved her from the death monster that took her sister.

Speaking softly, Gavin's mother went on. "I stayed in Dreamland with your father for a very long time, but it was impossible to tell hours from days from weeks. It felt like one extended dream to me. I created a better life here simply by wishing for it. Kinder parents. Sunnier days. More toys and friends and fun than I'd ever experienced. I imagined my sister with me, alive and walking and happy. But eventually, I grew weary of pretending. I wanted to wake up. To go home. Even if it meant returning to a bleaker reality without my sister."

When it fell silent for too long, Gavin realized no one wanted to share what happened next. So he asked, "Did you take her home, Father?"

There was no answer.

"Mother? Did you go home?"

She mumbled a reply. "I couldn't. It was too late."

Gavin glanced desperately between his parents, unable to meet either downcast gaze. He watched how their hands clasped tight to one another.

"Tell me why?" he finally insisted.

His father straightened up. With glistening eyes he explained. "Dreamers must wake every day to exercise and feed their bodies. Unlike ours, if their bodies are not fed, they eventually die."

Gavin's brow tightened. Quizzically, he looked to his mother. "But....but you're not dead."

Her shoulders involuntarily shrugged. "No, not *me*. But, my body.....the shell I use to live in......it died."

"But you're still here."

"Well, yes, I suppose."

Father spoke up. "As long as she stays here, your mother will live forever. No one dies in Dreamland, remember?"

Gavin nodded. This was a secret he'd always known. But only now did he truly understand its real meaning—its value. And here was a new secret, one he would need to ponder...

His own mother was a survivor from that other world. A refugee dreamer.

Taking the hands of both her son and her husband, Gavin's mother forced a smile, attempting to shove the past back where it belonged. "It's okay now. I have you and your father—two men I love dearly. I'm happy here now."

The little family turned their heads toward the podium when the hobbit-looking gentleman raised his voice, instructing the traveler to step down. This mysterious stranger had been speaking aloud to the assembly the whole time. Gavin had missed the traveler's tale. But judging by the sorrowful look on the man's face, the story must've sounded much like his father's, minus the semi-happy ending.

Chapter Six
Dreamers' Void

Parliament dismissed the entire assembly after concluding that more time was required to evaluate the matter. The key keeper received assurances his duties would remain solely his so long as no dreamers crossed into Dreamland. But the hobbitish man did stress the importance of informing parliament promptly if Gavin felt even slightly overwhelmed by the demands of his calling.

"Yes, your grace, I will certainly let you know if I need help."

Now you might think that after a full night of luring

away dreamers and ambushing pirates, followed by a stressful morning of council meetings, the young key keeper would be exhausted and seek out a few hours of restful slumber.   But here again is a secret most would consider enviable.

People in Dreamland don't require sleep.

Did I hear a laugh?   Silly—yes, I know.   To live in a place called Dreamland and never sleep!   What is that— ironical?   Paradoxical?   Regardless, it remains a fact.   I should elaborate here (so as not to cause confusion later on) that having no need for a good night's rest doesn't mean one *can't* sleep.   Virtually nothing is impossible in Gavin's world. Were he to desire sleep, he could slip into a peaceful, unconscious state with ease.   But as energetic and adventurous and curious as the young key keeper is, such a notion has never crossed his mind.   And so, instead of heading home after parliament, his determined strides took him once again outside the city gates.

Pausing within the short gap between Dreamland's ivy-covered walls and the surrounding dark forest, Gavin considered the unlikely and frankly shocking news about his mother.   He felt strange thinking about it, picturing her as an actual outsider, a dreamer, unwanted and deliberately barred from his world.   But what about his father who'd been a key keeper sworn to prevent dreamer's from entering their domain? He'd escorted one in!   *Invited* her!   Why?

Gavin recalled the excuse—the sorrow surrounding her sister's death.

Death.   What a brief word for the extinguishing of life. To *be* no more.   To have days cut off and at their end.   To never again.......anything.

It was hard for him to grasp the concept when his own

life sustained an opposite reality—one where there was always another day, another chance, another sunrise.

Apparently, the experience of witnessing death had been enough to overrule his father's loyalty to the duties he'd vowed to uphold. He'd reached out to a dreamer and pulled her inside. Saved her from nonexistence.

A warm feeling fell over the boy. A mix of security and comfort, as if a blanket were wrapping its soft layers around his heart and nuzzling him snuggly. Gavin loved his mother, and he would be forever grateful to his father for protecting her. The whole mystery behind it made him itch with curiosity, however.

Gavin took a determined step forward on a path partially concealed by drooping scrub brush. He rushed through the dark forest, knowing exactly where he was headed.

He made quick time reaching the opposite end of the woods, eventually entering a passageway formed by nothing more than two ongoing rows of facing, closed doors. Though temptations called invitingly from behind these exits, none were a lure for the key keeper. He would never reach to twist a devious knob. But to walk this hall meant an endless quest without a knowledge of how to escape it—another of the key keeper's secrets. A silly and simple one at that.

"Breathe in and blow, behold and lo, dispelled to mist the doors will go."

(Don't forget this rhyme. You might need it sometime.)

Gavin brought his palm below his lips as he sucked in a deep breath and held it. As if spreading magical pixie dust into the atmosphere, he blew every bit of air from his lungs over his upturned hand. The doors burst into a zillion, miniscule particles swept up by air currents that whirled and swirled, thickening the mist into a blinding shroud. Gavin stepped forward with sure faith until the mist cleared and his visibility returned. His footsteps halted, allowing him opportunity to scan the horizon.

Nothing.

Literally nothing could be seen where his eyes squinted to focus. It wasn't fog clouding the landscape or darkness hindering his sight. No, the fact was that nothing existed in the void; the great beyond; the outer limit. No light. No darkness. No tangible or visible matter. Nothing.

Gavin wondered why anyone would choose to wander this place. Why did travelers roam an area so lonely and desolate? His feet set to walking, assisting him in searching out the answer.

The lack of actual ground didn't hinder Gavin's ability to move forward. He advanced straight ahead as if crossing a stretch of desert plain, determined to get somewhere uncertain as quickly as possible. It was a flash of color, like a reflection off a shard of glass, that flickered in the corner of his eye, making his head turn and his progress falter. Where nothing had been a moment earlier, a game was suddenly taking place. A game of chess.

Curious, Gavin altered course and headed for a life-size, black-and-white checkerboard measuring eight spaces across and eight down, each a three-by-three foot square. His approach was unusually swift, as if the invisible ground beneath him sped in his direction at ten times the rate he moved forward. He stopped beside the board and watched two opponents—teens just older than himself dressed in decorated military attire—arrange their pieces in two lines facing off from either end of the board.

The first collection of chess pieces appeared to be made

from compacted bits of stone and gravel, ranging in heights, fashioned into assorted rock monsters. The second set of chess pieces were rubbery-smooth and glossy in appearance. Though the texture was appealing, the grotesque shapes— distorted faces and twisted forms—stirred up disturbing emotions in the observer.

"Excuse me," Gavin interrupted. The game hadn't yet begun. "What are you doing out here in the middle of nowhere?"

Only one of the decorated officers bothered to give a snappish answer. "What does it *look* like we're doing?"

Gavin gave the obvious reply. "Playing a game."

The teen scowled contemptibly and growled, "We're battling for possession of the Persmigony, you moron!"

More intrigued than offended, Gavin voiced another question. "What is the Persmigony?"

"Are you an absolute idiot? Do you know nothing of the keys to the kingdom?"

Gavin automatically put a hand to his heart—a guarded gesture toward the key beneath his shirt. "To what kingdom are you referring?"

With an indignant roll of the eyes, the young man offered a brief explanation. "The Persmigony grants a single chance at Charlmain's riddle. Correctly answering the riddle opens the sealed crypt where the key to the crown of Sire Quelmire awaits its new king. Possessor of that crown reigns over the kingdom of Farrenshire. Savvy?

"Well, I do now," Gavin huffed. Mumbling, he added, "Sounds like a tall tale to me."

"It isn't!" the officer spat, overhearing. "And neither are the giant trolls that guard Farrenshire's castle, keeping Princess Ruelle locked inside until the crown is claimed! But she won't be a prisoner much longer, because *I'm* going to win the crown *and* her hand *and* the throne!"

"Okay.   Good luck to you, then....I guess."

"I don't need your stinking luck."

Repelled by such a foul mood, Gavin walked to the opposite end of the game board.   His gaze remained behind, observing how the rock-and-gravel pawns were pushed into position, forming a short frontline.   Finding himself at the other corner, Gavin scanned two rows of milk-white chess pieces there.   A smooth, unblemished texture made them tempting to touch, yet the disturbing nature of their shapes stifled the urge.   A silent scowl from the second opponent deterred any attempt at conversation.

Eventually, both players took position among their own ranks, standing as chess pieces themselves in opposing squares normally reserved for the queens.

A piercing war cry bellowed from the lungs of each officer.   Gavin scuttled backwards, startled.   Magically, the game had come alive!

On one side, rock monsters made crunching noises with every bending limb.   The dark cement holding the stone creatures together burned and bubbled brilliant scarlet.   It looked like molten lava flowing between the conglomeratic rocks.   Gravel eyelids opened to reveal fiery holes for eyes. The ground trembled when the frontline of pawns stomped their boulder feet repeatedly on the game board.

Gavin's eyes darted to the other side where an army of milky, malleable figures crooked their backs, twisting and stretching their bodies in unnatural and unthinkable ways.   It was one freakish army challenging another.   Yet the key keeper understood that strategy alone determined the outcome in a game of chess.

A fair game, that is.

It took more time to gasp than it did to realize neither

side ever intended to play by the rules.   Though their pieces slid from square to square in moves resembling a proper chess game, no rhyme or reason controlled *when* they shifted, backward *or* forward.   There was no taking turns and no time to think.   War raged on the squared-off field, and only one apparent rule remained—governing *how* each piece slid across the board.   Other than that, it was a fierce battle of the strangest kind.   Rock-monsters used might and heaviness to plow into an opponent's piece only to meet elasticity.   The bendable figures seemed to absorb every ounce of force before springing it back on their attackers, sending stone figures flying across the board and crashing into piles of crumbling gravel. But their commanding officer—still standing in the queen's square, shielded by his most powerful pieces—ordered the pawns to reassemble and maintain a solid frontline.

"Burn them!" he shouted, his face as red as flames. "Burn them all!"

The rock monsters rose, and their gravely pieces magically realigned.   The lava plaster bonding their parts glowed brighter, flowing more fluidly between every crevice. Vaporous wisps rose from these hot spots, vanishing into the nothingness above their heads.   They moved forward, sliding and pausing momentarily within each square.

The first one to meet a pale rival hunkered down and growled.   As the lava within him appeared to liquefy and boil, his growl amplified into a thunderous roar.   The rock monster lunged forward.   Nearly shrouded in developing vapors, he rammed into a white enemy, indenting its putty form.   But this time the heat proved too much for the bendy figure. Instead of recoiling, the creature froze in that odd shape.   Its structure turned from flexible plastic to rigid porcelain—the transformation traveling swiftly from head to stump.   Another single hit shattered the porcelain statue into millions of sharp splinters.

A stunned, pale commander gaped at his demolished chess soldier, sensing lost hope for any miraculous resurrection. The battle was won swiftly from that point. When the ill-mannered teen stood haughtily triumphant, Gavin dared to meet his wild-eyed gaze.

"I am *victorious*! No one can stop me now! The Persmigony will reveal to me Charlmain's riddle, and I will solve it to earn the key to Sire Quelmire's crown! Farrenshire is as good as mine! Ruelle will be my queen, and we will rule from shore to shore!"

Before Gavin could offer a wise quip, the power-hungry victor vanished, along with his devastated checkerboard battlefield.

"Well—I imagine that will be unpleasant for just about everyone," the key keeper said to himself.

Distantly, another flash of movement caught his eye, followed by a frightened cry for mercy.

"No, no, stop! Please, don't! Please don't hurt me!"

The key keeper swiveled ninety degrees to face a faraway scene, not so remote that he couldn't make out a figure balled-up on the ground using two skinny arms as shields against a mob. Gavin stepped into a sprint and was carried instantly to the commotion.

"Back off!" he cried, wanting to stop what appeared to be a gang assault. The terrified face of a young boy turned up to him, gaunt and soil-stained. Hope for deliverance flickered in a pair of big brown eyes.

Gavin shifted focus, scanning a crowd of older kids who'd cornered the scrawny child against a fence. There were at least a dozen attackers, all wielding various make-shift weapons: baseball bats, shovels, two-by-fours, and raised fists clutching stones. He searched every face for an explanation.

"Does it seriously take the whole lot of you to harass one small defenseless boy?" All eyes glared in response to the cutting remark.

"This ain't none of ya bizzness, fool. Ya best turn tail an' git where ya came from, or we'll beat the life outta ya too, just like we gonna do with this rat fink here."

"Is that so?" Gavin took a step forward, gauging the overall reaction. No one moved or flinched except for the frightened schoolboy hugging the ground.

A bulky kid standing a foot above the rest shifted his stance enough to face off. He slapped a wooden bat in his open palm repeatedly.

"Ya deaf? In case ya din't hear me the firs time.....best be runnin' 'long, dimwit, or I'll pers'nally break ever last bone in ya body! Ya'll be lucky to slither off like a snake if I git holda ya."

A low, snickering murmur corroborated the threat.

"Let the boy go and I'll happily slither off," Gavin said.

The snickering increased in volume. A smirk twisted crookedly on the big kid's face. "That rat fink ain't none of ya concern. Now git 'long, curly! *Git!*"

Gavin didn't budge. The ring leader jerked his bat forward as if he would shove the key keeper with the end of it; he came shy of actually performing the task. No one flinched.

"Yer a stubborn cuss, ain't ya?"

Gavin tilted his head by a degree, prepared to offer a compromise. "I've a proposition for you bullies."

The boy curled his upper lip unattractively. "Eh?"

"Why not fight me first—all of you. Take *me* on, and anyone left standing can finish off the rat." He pointed to the skinny boy who cowered lower in response.

A few gang members shifted on their feet—a minor, anxious move.

"Got a death wish, do ya, dimwit?"

Gavin grinned impishly. "Can't pass up an opportunity for fun, that's all."

A few furtive glances were exchanged among the gang. Nervous glances.

At last, the big kid advanced a step, raising his bat in preparation to swing. "It's ya'lls funeral." His cronies, with readied weapons, followed suit.

The key keeper slapped his thighs, conjuring up two long swords which he swiftly pulled from their casings. Stunned expressions swept across the board, but the pack's momentum kept it pushing forward. Gavin ducked in time to hear a zip overhead— a wooden bat swung with acute force. In return, he lunged forward and sliced his blades through either sleeve on the big kid's upper arms. The move inflicted shallow gashes in the flesh, enough to draw blood. The bully howled at the pain, dropping his bat and covering wounds that quickly soaked his sleeves scarlet. The other boys looked to their leader and froze. Fear widened every stare.

Gavin straightened up and brought each sword high, leveling the steel with the ground. A devilish grin rounded his cheeks.

"Who's next?" he dared.

There was a raucous thud as makeshift weapons hit the dirt—handles, sticks, bats, rocks.....everything. Gavin pictured a stampede with how quickly the gang tore off, racing for safety elsewhere.

Teary-eyed and hugging himself, the biggest bully ran away last. "Hey! Wait fer me!"

Gavin watched the cowards vanish in a bright, thin burst of light. He then looked to the boy on the ground.

"It's okay. You can get up now, I'm not going to hurt you."

The child rose. He remained guardedly at a distance, shoulders raised, eyes wary and ashamed.

"Thank you," he mumbled.

"You're welcome." Gavin's brows tilted, observing how scared the boy continued to appear. He wished his swords away, hoping to ease apprehensions. "Are you going to be okay?"

The timid boy shook his head.

Gavin glanced around, finding no further threat. "Can I do anything to help you?"

Again, the little boy shook his head. In a near whisper he said, "They pick on me when I'm awake. I wish they didn't haunt my dreams too."

It was instinctual to step forward—part of his nature to offer compassion. The key keeper simply wanted to share his secret…

…that dreams belong to the dreamer only.

But the frightened child vanished before Gavin could explain how to focus and alter a nightmare. Gavin stared at the spot where a slit of light flashed and swallowed up the boy.

"Poor kid," he sighed.

Moving on, he swept the horizon with his eyes from right to left. Nothing. Then he scanned the void again from left to right. Far, far away a blip of color blemished the emptiness. He headed for it, curious to behold another dreamer's visions.

His approach halted at the very edge of a wooded area where trees stood tall and densely packed. It was obvious this imagined forest was meant to spread for acres and acres, but in this dream only a portion of trees appeared at any time. They existed around the footsteps of a young girl.

The key keeper kept his presence hidden at first, watching from behind a cluster of stick-straight, white oaks. His eyes followed the girl whose skin appeared nearly as pale as the trees. She dashed from one hiding place to the next, her long raven waves lifting and falling with every hurried move. Her clothing was a plain lavender dress that reached to her knees. She wore no shoes.

Dashing from tree cover to a sizable boulder, the girl checked behind her for something or someone. It was evident she feared a pursuer. Gavin moved stealthily until he was at her back. He stooped low and spoke softly.

"*Shhh*, I won't hurt you."

She jumped nonetheless, jerking her head to stare wide-eyed at a stranger. Her eyes—rich pools of chocolate brown saturated with fright—caught the key keeper off guard. The look stole his breath.

"I won't hurt you," he assured her again.

The drumming in her chest seemed to settle with his reassurance.

"Are you alright?" he asked.

The girl stole a glance past their rock hiding place.

"Three bears," she said. "They're chasing me. I think I made them mad."

"How? What did you do?"

"I ate their porridge and broke one of their chairs and slept in one of their beds."

Gavin's face screwed up. "Why?"

The girl shrugged, glancing again at where she'd come from. "Because that's the way the story goes."

A twig snapped loudly, grabbing both their attention. "The bears!" she exclaimed. "They're coming!"

She took off running. Gavin followed. Fresh forest appeared before their every rapid stride. A beastly growl shook the air and the girl squealed.   She picked up the pace. The key keeper tried calling to her.

"Wait!   Wait!   You're not in any danger!"

Her flight didn't slow in the least.   She didn't believe him.

Gavin's legs were longer, however, and enabled him to catch up.   He caught her by the arm and pulled her close, both of them ducking behind an especially thick tree trunk.   Her rich brown eyes gleamed with alarm as she stared up at him questioningly.   A long strand of black hair crossed over the bridge of her nose.

"You're not....in danger," he panted.   "You don't need....to run from bears."

"But they'll eat me!" she worried.

Gavin brushed the hair off her nose, away from her face.   A tiny smile tugged at the corners of his mouth.   "It's okay, I promise."

Her eyebrows—as pitch black as the long waves framing her face—skewed skeptically.   "I don't think you're right.   You don't know how the story goes."

"What story?"

"*The Three Bears!*"

He made a baffled expression.   "I've never heard of it, but I do know being swallowed by a bear doesn't hurt.   It's actually..."

His words were cut off by a vicious growl and a high-pitched shriek.   A black bear standing as tall as a house appeared from around the corner with his claws raised and mouth open wide.   The girl yanked her arm free and turned to run.   All of a sudden, there was a blinding flash as a thin tear opened up in midair.   The girl disappeared within the light. Her fantasy of three pursuing bears was erased.

Gavin stood alone, suspended in an empty void once

again.   He felt frightened for the first time.   A strong desire had overcome him for a brief moment—a yearning to follow that girl, to chase her into the light.   He'd nearly been moved to do so.   Only a moment of hesitation—not knowing the outcome—had managed to separate them.   What if he had shadowed that raven-haired creature into her world, what would've happened?   Who would've guarded the gates of Dreamland with him gone?

   With haste and an uneasy exhale the key keeper started directly for home.

Chapter Seven
Ogre Bowl

There is a favorite spot inside the borders of Dreamland where the young key keeper likes to sit and pucker his brow while doing his most serious thinking. This quiet, out-of-the-way place provides an amazing view that stretches well beyond the city gates. Being located so very high above sea level (and above cloud level) this chilly, bare bit of land is usually only visited by individuals who commonly fly, like pixies, firebirds, dragons, whisperers, and such.

On this particular day Gavin found himself

accompanied by a ghostly whisperer who was also seeking solitude.   The pair dangled their legs over a pointed peak, seated side by side upon the slope of a luminous crescent moon.   Their focus was on all of Dreamland spread out far below.   Leaning against one another's shoulder, they discussed the key keeper's concerns.

"Do you know what's out there.....beyond the forest and the trails?"   Gavin gestured toward the bleak distance in question—the void he'd just returned from.

"There's nothing out there.   Nothing significant, anyway.   Only dreamers and mad travelers."

Gavin glanced up sideways at the figure beside him. "Why do you call them mad?"

The whisperer made a single, humorless chuckle. "Because they wander around empty space chasing after figures that appear and disappear with no rhyme or reason. They try to make sense where there is none.   It's crazy madness!   Lunacy!   What else would you call it?"

Gavin shrugged his free shoulder.   "Curiosity maybe?"

The whisperer jostled slightly with another weak chuckle.   The key keeper caught a glimpse of a contrary expression.

"Aren't you even a little bit curious?   Don't you wonder about dreamers?   Who they are?   What they want? Where they disappear to?"

The whisperer shook his head.   "I know all I need to know about them.   They're a selfish and greedy lot, wanting anything and everything you have.   They're bad news.   I don't care where it is they go, so long as they disappear far away from Dreamland."

Gavin thought of his mother.   He thought of the cowering, scrawny boy and the raven-haired girl who even now made his lips smile just picturing her.   "I don't think they're all bad."

The whisperer voiced no reply.

It was silent for a while excepting the eerie whistle of a cool breeze that twisted around the moon as if the wind were an invisible, orbiting ring. Clouds rolled in far below their dangling feet, curtaining off the view of Dreamland. Eventually, the key keeper spoke up again. He muttered a confession.

"I went out there."

Gavin waited for his companion to comment. When silence persisted, the key keeper spoke again.

"I went alone. I saw things. Strange things."

"Unimportant things," the whisperer said in a low grumble. "What in the world made you want to step foot in dreamers' territory?"

Gavin's forehead tightened. "I suppose I was curious. I just….well…I wanted to know…" His words cut off for a number of reasons. Mainly, he wasn't sure exactly what he was searching for. His mother had once dreamt among those who appeared and vanished in that void. He needed to understand it. Not all of it, but a piece that might help him define her.

There was also a legitimate concern this whisperer couldn't be trusted with his mother's secret. He was unsure if others knew about her origin. Gavin understood it was part of a whisperer's job to persuade intruders to leave Dreamland. Would they hold a grudge against her if they learned the truth?

"You have questions about your mom," the whisperer said. His words answered the young man's thoughts, making the key keeper wonder if his companion was also a mind reader.

Gavin nodded assuredly in reply.

"Your mom's a good soul, one of us now. We were

lucky with her in that way. She's buried her past, and you should too. Let it go, boy. Stay away from the void. Keep near the gates and do your job. It'll drive you mad otherwise, like it has the travelers. Like it nearly did your father. He's not been back out there since he brought your mother home."

Gavin looked up to find a stern face worrying down at him.

"Heed my words, key keeper. Steer clear of dreamers. Chase them off. Don't let one snare you."

Though his head moved up and down agreeably, just the thought of that brown-eyed girl was enough to weaken any resolve to never step foot in the void again. Gavin couldn't help think his mother may have been just like that girl once.

The two companions realized they were no longer alone on their iridescent moon rest. A gathering of pixies was moving in, their thin wings flitting at hummingbird speed. The tiny figures zipped here and there in a swarm, buzzing about excitedly.

"Come play with us! Come down from the moon and play!"

The key keeper straightened up, eager to hear what the pixies had in mind. He welcomed a distraction from his latest concerns.

"Come, Gavin! An ogre is in the valley bowling! All the children are there, including the elves and sprites and gnomes…"

"And us too!" declared a silver pixie, grinning so wide his dimpled cheeks nearly touched his ears.

"Yes, yes, us too!" the others agreed. "Come and play! An ogre is bowling!"

The key keeper smiled in a lopsided way and hopped right off the edge of his seat, catching himself by one hand on the pointed tip of the moon. Every tiny member in the cloud of pixies zipped over to take hold of the young man. They lifted him away, flying him safely down to a stretch of green valley far below.

The very moment he was standing on two feet again, Gavin hustled across the grass to join a throng of other young characters. They were all shuffling about, making sure not to keep in one spot for too long. All eyes were glued on the colossal form shadowing them. Gavin crooked his neck to look up, noting the ogre's big nose first. It was as round and red and shiny as a tomato, matching the fat lips frowning beneath it. The ogre's head reflected sunlight, bald as an eagle. He was a sore sight to behold—a gruesome, overstuffed Goliath—and his foul mood didn't improve this first impression the least bit.

Like all the others gathered to have fun, the young key keeper kept outside of the ogre's reach, his feet constantly in step. Which direction the group shuffled was dependent upon the ogre's moves. One great stride to the right sent the throng of tiny people hustling left. Advancing forward drove them backwards, and so on. When multiple attempts to chase down and scoop up a handful of children failed, (the poor ogre was too pot-bellied to possess speed enough to catch even a gnome) the grouchy giant stomped over to a pair of items he'd carted to the valley with him.

One was a bird cage.

The other a bowling ball.

Both were his size.

Jamming two fat fingers and a thumb into a triangle of drilled holes, the ogre lifted the bowling ball up to his chest. He let it rest on his protruding stomach, rounded in much the same shape. Sounds of amusement rose from children who noticed the similarity.

The ogre scowled with disdain. A growl rumbled

from deep in his gut while the length of his forearm wiped beneath a red, swollen nose, catching a string of slimy snot that stuck to his skin. Those watching groaned, disgusted. But when the ogre let his hand fall to swing the bowling ball backwards, a gasp chorused from the group. Everyone not hovering above the ground stood on tiptoe, ready.

The ogre grunted and took a step forward. Using an underhanded swing he released the bowling ball, aiming for the middle of the crowd. Tens of tiny feet ran left. Tens more hustled right. The ball shot straight through the center gap and rolled to a dead stop.

A frustrated grumble crossed the giant's lips as Gavin and the others cheered their success at avoiding being bowled over. The ground shook when the ogre started across the grass to retrieve his ball. But when he stopped after only a few steps, all eyes looked up at him. The grumpy giant was staring off—smiling. He snorted on an unexpected laugh. Gavin followed the ogre's line of sight across the valley, seeing in the distance a second Goliath headed their way making very fast time.

A loud murmur of conversation started up immediately—excited talk of how the pace and the challenge would double with *two* ogres bowling!

Gavin turned to the person beside him, a blonde boy with sapphire eyes who wore a silver breast plate over his shirt.

Gavin pointed to the decorated metal on his chest. "Does that help? The armor, I mean."

The boy nodded. "Sure does. Makes it less painful if you get caught."

Gavin lifted a questioning eyebrow beneath his curly bangs. "Have you been caught many times?"

"Five times."

"Twice, myself."

"Stings like a scorpion, don't it?"

Gavin grinned knowingly. "Yeah, it sure does."

The two boys ended their conversation as soon as they realized the second ogre had reached their stretch of valley. This giant stood even taller than the first, with a portly belly to match. He had a full head of hair, however, and a honker that looked more like a stubby, twisted carrot stick than a tomato.

Picking up the bowling ball, the second ogre gained everyone's undivided attention. The crowd who had split apart at the first throw now came together to form a massive group of living pins. On tiptoe they waited for the giant's next move. Sprites and pixies hovered over the other youngsters, anxiously flitting their wings.

Taking three leading steps that shook the ground, the ogre sent the bowling ball whizzing in a straight line. It crooked to the right at the very last second; he'd added a tricky twist to his throw! Screams pierced the air as the majority of the crowd veered left, but those who dodged right were caught in the throes of danger. The curve ball followed their frantic dash. A puff of pixies and sprites scattered into the air, a few daring to pause long enough to snatch a non-flying child out of the line of fire.

"Hurry, hurry, run!"

"Move!"

"Watch out!"

"Duck!" shouted those who witnessed the danger.

Not everyone managed to jump aside, and a line of bodies were flattened like pancakes. The ogres wasted no time hustling over to scoop up those who couldn't rise quickly enough. The unfortunate were tossed into a large birdcage and locked away for later.

And so the game went on in this manner, a throng of children playing keep-away from a bowling ball tossed back and forth between two plump ogres.   The air filled with shrieks and cheers and shouts of laughter as daring players thrilled at the sport.   That is, all but the few poor souls knocked flat and captured.   No laughter rose from behind bars because those in the birdcage knew what was in store.   They would soon be lunch for a couple of hungry ogres.

Now you might be thinking—didn't Gavin call it fun when he was swallowed by a wolf earlier?   And didn't he tell that raven-haired girl it doesn't hurt to be swallowed whole by a bear?   All true, all true.   But here's a secret you might not know.

Ogres chew their food.

Luckily, it's only the first bite that stings.

Chapter Eight
Prince Lyarg

An iridescent sliver of moon traveled across the sky and vanished before darkness consumed a ruby-red sunset.   Having managed to steer clear of every ogre-thrown bowling ball, the young key keeper made his way home by starlight.   He'd had a fun evening with the ogres. Avoiding them anyway.

Entering his house and noting the dim lighting, Gavin quietly stepped around to the front room.   There he found his father seated on the sofa, nose-in-book, reading under the soft yellow light of a table lamp.   His wife was resting her head on his lap, her dark hair an entangled pillow beneath her cheek. She was asleep, her body stretched out across the length of sofa.   Gavin's father made a gesture of silence as soon as he noticed his son.   He put down his book and motioned for the boy to enter the room.   The two conversed in near whispers.

"How are you, son?"

"Fine, Father."

Gavin half-leaned, half-sat on the free arm of the occupied seat.   His eyes fell on his mother, regarding how peacefully she slept.   Sleeping was something he nor his father ever did, both considering it a needless waste of time. Gavin had never understood his mother's practice of daily slumber—her insistence to block out the world behind closed eyes for a period.   And yet he'd never really questioned it either......until now.   Realizing her secret—that she was a dreamer—explained a lot.   It made sense she'd be different. A grave question interrupted Gavin's moment of contemplation.

"Son, I hope your opinion of your mother hasn't lessened, knowing what you now know."

Gavin glanced up; incredulity skewed his eyebrows. His expression appeared both stunned and appalled.   "Never, Father!   I love her!   It makes no difference to me where she came from."

The man nodded, a show of relief softening his features.   His large hand went to brush a string of hair away from his wife's peaceful profile.   "Your mother loves you too, son, more than anything in the world.   She worries about you, day and night."

That sentiment stirred something profoundly pleasant inside the boy.   He grinned at the internal warmth it created.

"We both love you, son."

"I know, Father."

Together they looked down at the sleeping woman. There was a moment of silence followed by a tentative sigh.

"I uh….I suppose you have questions."

Gavin's eyes flickered up again, meeting a face tight with concern. His father forced a weak smile.

The boy nodded automatically. Of course he wanted to know more, but it was difficult to know what to ask; where to begin? Gesturing with his head at his mother, he questioned the observable.

"Why does she sleep? Is that something all dreamers do?"

"Of course, son, you already know that. Dreamers enter our realm when they're fast asleep. That's when they have their visions."

Gavin nodded. "Right, but why does she still do it? She doesn't need to now, does she?"

"No, it's no longer necessary, but she finds comfort in the routine. I suppose you could call it a peaceful habit from her preexistence. She enjoys her sleep."

Gavin still didn't understand. What was the fun in just lying there doing nothing? Perceiving nothing?

His father smiled, understanding his son's confusion. "It makes her happy, Gavin."

"It seems strange to me," the boy admitted with a shrug.

His father's smile widened, humored. "And to her, purposefully falling on the sword of Captain Drake Blackmont seems strange."

Gavin rolled his eyes and made a face that caused his father to laugh. They each shushed the other when the slumbering woman stirred.

Seeing how his mother's eyes remained closed and her breathing steady, Gavin dared another question. "Do you think travelers are mad? I mean, you've been out there, Father, right? You've seen how dreamers are. Will being around one for too long drive a person mad?"

His father's head was shaking before Gavin even finished the question. "No, no, no, son. Dreamers won't drive you mad. Otherwise you and I would be as loony as they come! Travelers are....well...they're curious and caring souls. They're determined and...uh....I'm not sure how to explain it." A furrow creased between his brows as the old key keeper tried to put his understanding into words. "It can be a painstaking experience to follow a dreamer and become familiar with one. Their problems are harder to solve than ours. It's.......frustrating."

"Is that why you don't go out there anymore?"

The man frowned. He placed a gentle hand over his wife's ear and whispered, "It is heartrending to become close to someone only to lose her, Gavin. It's a pain you never get over."

Staring into eyes glistening with genuine sorrow, Gavin went to nod at such solemn words. But a glowing key beckoned him, emanating from beneath the young man's shirt. His father understood its meaning immediately.

"Go, son—go on now. See to the gates. Protect Dreamland."

The young key keeper was reluctant to leave. He hadn't finished with his questions yet, but urgency moved him. If an outsider were to find a way in, the whisperers would be summoned.

Gavin hustled from home to the high, white walls surrounding his city. He knew exactly where to go, guided by the key. Standing just inside the gates, he waved a hand over the ground. A nonsensical phrase fell from his lips—words possessing magic.

"Sillasun Laddrius Flur!"

The spell caused a small area to rumble at his feet. This spot of soil swelled, forming a tiny hill before crumbling away to allow a sunflower to push through. The plant grew swiftly, reaching higher than the stone wall. Its structure was as solid as a metal pole. Sturdy leaves created steps for the key keeper to climb. Halfway up, he was able to spy over the ivy-laden gates.

"Ah-hah!" he grinned. "Peek-a-boo, I see you."

On the forest ground below stood a trio of siblings that appeared near his age. They were dressed in grubby shirts rolled up at the sleeves and tattered jeans fastened by suspenders. Turned-about baseball caps covered all three of their tousled hair-dos. Gavin was surprised to find out the shortest and bossiest character was a girl.

Thrusting out her lower lip, this pony-tailed female blew hard, lifting a long mess of dusty-blonde bangs out of her eyes. With a fist planted on each hip, she barked out orders to her brothers who were slouched behind her. Both boys appeared to outrank their sister in age which made it truly bizarre to see them jump at her command.

"Tug on those vines, Henry; see if they'll hold any weight. Oliver, give me a lift up. Don't let go until I say. And stay under me, you hear? I'll sock the both of you if I hit the ground—and don't think I won't!"

The brothers nodded in sync. "Alright, Sissy." They moved to do exactly as they'd been told.

Gavin realized the girl's intent was to scale the wall. He thought of a plan to stop her and quickly went about it. By making a single wish, the key keeper transformed himself into a dark creature—half-man, half-beast. Long, taut wings folded compactly on his back. In gargoyle form he leapt onto the stone divider and grasped it with clawed feet. He sidestepped along the top, stopping directly above all three siblings.   A warning growl gurgled up from his gut, catching their attention.   One glance at him sent the three skittering backwards.   It was Sissy who stopped her brothers from turning tail to run.

"Wait, wait, you guys!   This is a dream, Henry! Oliver, that thing ain't real.   It can't hurt us in a dream."

The boys turned back, hesitant.   The girl marched forward, determined to prove she was right.

"Get over here, Oliver, and lift me up like I told you!"

The boy complied; although, his eyes remained steadfast on the gruesome gargoyle looming overhead.   He clasped his trembling fingers together and offered a lift to his sister.

"Hurry up, Sissy."

She stepped onto his hands and reached for the vines as he hoisted her up.

"That ugly watchdog don't scare me," she grumbled under her breath.   "I'm gonna find out what he's guarding behind this wall."

Attempting again to scare off the intruders, Gavin spread his beastly wings, stretching them high and wide.   He roared ferociously.   Oliver stumbled over his feet hustling to where Henry hugged the tree line.   Sissy lost her grip on the vines and fell to the ground with a grunt.

"You stupid, ugly dog!   You're nothin' but a dream!" she shouted up at the creature.

Hoping to convince them otherwise, the key keeper swooped down from his perch and soared over the heads of Henry and Oliver.   They hit the ground, terrified, shrieking like toddlers.   Both boys balled up to avoid being grazed by razor-sharp claws.   When the gargoyle disappeared above the trees, Henry jumped to his feet and took off running.   Oliver had the same idea, but paused when Sissy bellowed at him.

"You cowards! Big babies! Haven't you any manhood at all?"

Oliver pivoted to look at the girl, his heart visibly pounding in his chest. It was clear by his expression her words had wounded him, and he went to defend himself.

"That thing could shred us to pieces, Sissy! That monster went after *us!* Not you, but me and Henry! You saw it!"

She regarded him firmly—fearlessly. "It ain't real, Oliver. No *man* would run from shadows. I promise you it's just a dream." Her stare demanded he believe her.

The young man seemed to waver, considering valor versus his personal wellbeing. When he finally made his choice, his heels inched backwards. "If this is just a dream then none of it matters anyway. I'm not sticking around to see it turn into a bloody nightmare!"

And then he was gone.

Sissy hollered at the trees. "Fine, you big baby! Run away! Go find your mommy!"

Breathing deep, the girl squared her shoulders and raised her chin high. She turned to the wall, undaunted, and pulled herself up by tugging on a thick bundle of vines. She managed to scale a third of the wall before a voice she didn't recognize called out her name.

"Sissy! Sissy, stop! What are you doing? Have you lost your mind?"

Holding tight to her ivy rope, she cricked her neck to look down over a shoulder. She was surprised to find a tall, slender, curly-haired boy staring up at her with big brown eyes. His expression appeared to be one of genuine concern.

"Who are you?" she called down.

"My name is Gavin. Who are you?"

"You already said my name. Now tell me, how'd you

come by it?"

Gavin stepped up to the wall so the girl could see him more easily. "I passed your brothers in the forest. They told me about you and what you were doing. I said if it was true you'd be a daft one. So I had to come see for myself if there was indeed a real fool scaling Prince Lyarg's gates. And what do I find? An honest-to-goodness ignorant fool!"

Sissy glowered at the boy looking up at her. "I'm no fool! My brothers are cowards! *That's* the truth!"

Gavin laughed aloud, causing the girl's face to turn anger-red. He beckoned for her to come down, but she refused. "You're not going to stop me either!"

"Fine, Sissy, just answer this before you throw your life away. Is it cowardly to protect yourself from being turned into a hideous gargoyle? Or worse, turned into a mindless slave after being captured by Prince Lyarg?"

Sissy's red face twisted up with uncertainty. "What are you talking about?"

"If you come down, I'll explain." Gavin glanced at the forest with a serious look of concern. "But you should move quickly before that gargoyle returns."

The girl narrowed her eyes as if annoyed by the whole thing, but she climbed down a ways and jumped safely to the ground. Sissy purposefully kept distanced from the boy who was a stranger to her.

Gavin moved away from the wall. "We should seek cover in the trees."

Sissy failed to follow his lead. "No. Not until you explain yourself. What did you mean by being changed into a gargoyle?"

"Or a slave," Gavin repeated. He moved closer to the girl until she lifted a halting hand. There he stopped to share a story.

"You see, Sissy, there's a secret behind that wall. A dark and terrible one. On the other side lies a kingdom belonging to a heartless ruler known as Prince Lyarg. He has powers he abuses to control and possess people. He can fog their minds and keep them spellbound eternally. Prince Lyarg controls an army of flying creatures as well. We call them gargoyles, but in reality they're actually young men like your brothers who've been transformed into hideous monsters that do the bidding of their master. This is the fate of all boys who fall into Prince Lyarg's hands."

Sissy glanced at the trees as if looking with concern for her brothers. The story didn't stop there.

"It's far worse for the girls who are captured. Those young pretty things become slaves to the prince. One look into his eyes and their minds are lost forever. No one knows how to break the trance he places over those poor darlings. They behave as if they adore him, even to the point of returning to his arms after being rescued by their own family members. It's a sad and frightful thing, Sissy. Dreadfully frightful. If that gargoyle had gotten ahold of you or your brothers, it would've taken you directly to Prince Lyarg. An awful fate awaits the fool who crosses over that wall."

Sissy's big eyes darted back and forth between Gavin and the stone wall. She seemed worried and nervous, but also disbelieving. "This is just a dream," she insisted. "All of it's nothin' more than a dream."

Gavin agreed without hesitation. "Yes, it is."

The girl grinned at his assent, finding a bit of backbone again. "Then I have absolutely nothing to worry about."

But Gavin's stare intensified in response to her false assumption. His head shook assuredly back and forth. In a low and serious tone he shared his biggest secret of all.

"Understand this, Sissy...

Dreams.   Are.   Real.

That's why they affect you, often forcefully.   Some dreams have the power to keep you from ever waking up again. Are you willing to take that chance?"

With a countenance suddenly as pallid as the stone wall beside her, Sissy shook her head.   Her focus turned to the trees.   "I want to go home."

"Go on," Gavin urged the frightened dreamer.   "Run fast, and don't turn back."

The key keeper watched her scamper away.   Then he leaned against the gates of Dreamland and crossed his arms triumphantly.   His lips spread into a puckish grin as he congratulated himself on another successful intervention. Okay, so maybe he'd had to conjure up a tall tale about a fictitious evil prince to do the job, but the result had been winning.   Dreamers aren't the only ones with imagination, you know.

Chapter Nine
Brown Eyes

I should probably tell you a thing or two about Dreamland's young key keeper. More specifically about the calling itself. It ought to be apparent by now that this position, held by a single individual, is highly esteemed. There's no age requirement for the job. A candidate must simply be a citizen of Dreamland, chosen by the former key keeper. For this reason—given that the responsibility as well as the coveted key is handed down without election—the calling has belonged primarily to those within generations of the same family.

For example, Gavin's father presented the key to his

son shortly after the boy began seeking adventures away from home. The key had previously passed through the hands of all of Gavin's great-grandfathers up to the fifth great. But this pattern wasn't always followed. The fact is, when an existing key keeper chooses to give up his calling, he has the right to turn the key over to anyone he deems worthy—anyone at all. It could be a son or daughter, a friend, a neighbor, or even a notorious pirate. Parliament officially swears in the new key keeper and presents him (or her) to the public. It is then a done deal.

Now, you might be thinking that a great amount of trust and power are granted to a key keeper. That is so. But rest assured, parliament does retain the right to dismiss anyone from the position if the action is warranted. The decision would require a unanimous vote among the heads of parliament. And wo be to the poor key keeper discharged in such a way. A personal disgrace! Near unbearable!

Just for the record; it has never happened.

It's perhaps interesting to note that only one authentic key has ever been formed. No tangible copy exists. Yet there *are* copies—intangible ones, few and far between—capable of opening the front gates.

I've got your attention, have I? Let me explain another secret then.

It is a key keeper's right to bestow a copy of his key on anyone he wishes.

But this practice—a phenomenal rite—is hardly ever performed. To receive a copy of the key means to have its imprint seared into your hand. Holding that branded replica over the front lock miraculously parts the gates to Dreamland. It works just as effectively as inserting the genuine key.

Staggering to think about, isn't it?   You might consider clenching your fists when you dream.

Well now, back to Gavin.

After having successfully driven off Sissy, Henry, and Oliver, Gavin felt an anxious desire to hurry home and resume questioning his father.   There were facts and details he continued to wonder about.   Though the young man had often crossed paths with roaming dreamers outside the gates, he actually knew little of the world in which they came from.   It was a place where death lurked unseen and feared.   And it was a harsh, non-magical land.   These facts he'd learned. His father had visited the dreamers' world which meant it was possible for Gavin to do likewise.

The very thought sent a shiver crawling down the key keeper's spine.   He shoved himself away from the wall, determined to rush home and seek answers to the forming notions in his mind.

Starting for the front gate, a flash of movement stopped him in his tracks; he caught a glimpse of someone ducking in the woods across the way.   Gavin stared at the spot.   For a moment he thought it might be a guardian—but no.   Shadow monsters were expert at remaining both motionless and silent unless prepared to leap out and frighten someone.   Just to be sure, Gavin called to the guardians, speaking in monster tongue.

"Graaa graaa!   Gerrrr!   *Rrrroooaaar!*"

No answer came, but the spot of greenery he'd been watching shook with sudden movement.   Gavin wondered if his simulation of a beastly growl had spooked someone. Another dreamer perhaps?

He took off after the shadow.   "Who's there?" he called, ducking into the woods.   It crossed his mind that Sissy might've returned.   Perhaps she'd seen through his fabricated story. "Wait up! Who's there?"

Gavin zipped around the trees, following a trail of swaying underbrush and shuddering branches. He was fast closing in when a glimpse of the fleeing culprit caught his eye. The form clearly suggested a young girl. He saw only her back—not Sissy's blonde tangles as expected but long waves as black as a crow.

He was instantly overcome by the recent memory of wide, chocolate-brown eyes staring up at him. Could this possibly be the same girl?

Wanting to know for certain, he deliberately hurried his pace. "Wait up!" he called out with greater desperation. "Wait! Wait, I won't hurt you!"

The frightened creature failed to submit to his pleas, speeding up her own steps and jumping behind every timber as she led her pursuer on a zigzagged chase. Owning the longer stride, however, Gavin soon drew near and stopped the girl by the arm. She screamed at his grip and yanked hard in hopes of freeing herself.

Her neck crooked and two teary eyes looked up at the key keeper.

Blue eyes. Not brown.

"No," Gavin sighed, showing his disappointment. How startling to him that his heart would groan so potently.

His grip fell slack, and he allowed the girl to pull away. She stumbled backwards, tripped, and fell.

The child bawled, "Leave me alone! I want to go home!"

Compassion moved the key keeper to squat down to her level. He offered a warm smile and calm assurances. "It's okay, it's okay. I can help you get home. I know a short cut out of here."

He extended a hand to assist her up, but the girl shied

away. She scrambled to her feet on her own, putting extra space between this stranger and herself. There she waited as if agreeing to follow him.

Gavin rose slowly to his full height. "Come along. I'll lead you to your door."

The blue-eyed girl kept her distance but nodded.

Wiping at tear-stained cheeks, she walked behind the key keeper while the surrounding forest blurred and distorted. When their surroundings refocused, it became an extended hall of varied exits. Gavin kept one eye over his shoulder to see the girl gawk at this magical transformation.

They proceeded forward at a snail's pace, allowing time for individual doors of interest to be examined. A few the girl approached. Others she strained an ear toward, curious about muffled sounds coming from the opposite side. Eventually, one particular barrier worked its magic, painting a smile of recognition on the girl's face and visibly relaxing her entire countenance. Hurried steps brought her within arm's length of a brass knob which she reached out to twist and tug before vanishing in the doorway.

Gavin had lured another dreamer away from his homeland and diverted her through a portal to her own world. But the key keeper didn't pause to bask in his accomplishment. He didn't turn for Dreamland to seek out his father whom moments ago he'd longed to bombard with questions. The young man's strides failed to slacken even a little as he traveled further and further down a never-ending hall of doors.

The fact was, Gavin had had an epiphany. While chasing after that lost girl, it occurred to him his father's knowledge about dreamers had been obtained firsthand through observation on their turf. Where his father might not suitably answer all of his questions, experience undoubtedly would. Thinking about it convinced him more and more no better way existed of discovering what he wished to know.

The key keeper continued forward, resolute in his aim, telling himself what he sought was knowledge and understanding. But the image he couldn't seem to shake from his mind was of two big, brown eyes painted on a milky complexion. He needed to know more. About dreamers. About her.

Gavin brought his palm to his lips and blew a deep breath of air across his open hand. And, of course, you can guess what happened next. Remember the rhyme? The one you might need sometime? Yes, yes, that's it! Say it with me now…

"Breathe in and blow, behold and lo, dispelled to mist the doors will go."

And that's exactly what happened. The endless hall of mystical entries and exits smeared into vapor as thick as swamp fog. Blindness didn't hinder the key keeper's advance, however. He strode forward, guided by faith. When the mist parted and his sight returned, the effect on his senses remained comparable to blindness, for there was naught in existence to be perceived. His footsteps came to a halt within the dreamers' void.

He scanned the emptiness. Nothing. Again his eyes swept an expanse devoid of both darkness and light. Still nothing registered. Believing that a dreamer must be out there somewhere, Gavin thrust one foot forward and then the other, performing the act of walking without the support of ground on which to set the soles of his boots. Lacking any sense of bearing—whether he traveled up, down, left, or right—the key keeper moved on in search of a dreamer.

Finally, when he'd nearly alarmed himself into

believing oblivion had swallowed him whole, Gavin caught a splash of brilliant color in the distance. He rushed towards it, reaching the scene in impossibly quick time.

A portion of spring meadow appeared, bathed in bright, warm, golden sunshine. Two girls in frilly, pastel jumpers held butterfly nets high in the air as they skipped through a dale of long grasses and wildflowers. Honey-colored braids draped over their shoulders and bounced with every hop. Tiny, white butterflies flitted everywhere, enough to be swooped up by each lazy swish of a net. High-pitched, giggly trills accompanied their play. It was a beautiful scene. A beautiful dream.

The key keeper set foot in the tall grass and watched. He yearned to join the fun and dared a few strides further into the meadow. The tallest of both playmates noticed him first. She stopped abruptly to stare, all expression of bliss drained completely from her face. Gavin smiled wide hoping the girl might rediscover her own smile, but her eyebrows knit together in a look of concern.

Gavin reached out to catch a handful of butterflies. He then held his fist high as a sign of success. The smaller girl noticed him then, and her gleeful expression fizzled away. She gave the young man a wary regard, her untrusting gaze darting back and forth between his raised fist and the tentative smile on his lips. When he opened his fingers to reveal the captured butterflies, instead of miniature white wings flitting up and away, the poor things tumbled from his palm—dead.

Both girls screamed, horrified, and ran off in the other direction. A dazzle of light flickered as a fissure appeared and engulfed them. The meadow and thousands of white butterflies disappeared as well.

Gavin stood alone in the void.

"Sorry," he breathed to no one.

He sighed dismally, feeling bad for what he'd unintentionally done. But it did no good apologizing to himself. A quick look around presented another scene to consider anyway. Gavin started off again, more cautiously this time, toward what appeared to be a flat expanse of green turf in the distance.

A pack of boys had gathered in an open park, all young enough to appreciate a rough and rowdy game of junior football. Excitement buzzed in the air as they chattered in chorus, a few distinct voices speaking more loudly over the whole. There were shouts of approval mixed with groans of disappointment, all noise rising from the list of names called out by those deciding teams. One by one the group separated into two—shirts vs. skins.

An old leather football appeared from beneath the armpit of a self-appointed quarterback. He tossed the ball straight into the air and then stretched his arms out on either side of him, motioning for everyone to step back.

"Call it!" he ordered.

The rival quarterback decided swiftly. "Heads! We call heads!"

The ball hit the grass, flipped, rolled, and then wobbled to a stop. A circle of faces huddled to stare down at the leather casing. On the curved side up was a fairly good likeness of a rabbit's backside fixed with a big, fluffy tail; it was drawn in black permanent marker.

"Hah! It's tails!"

Shirts won the first drive. Skins formed a defensive line.

Gavin remained at a discreet distance to observe the game. Shirts proved the better team, possessing taller players and faster sprinters. Having a quarterback with a swift spiral aimed accurately on ninety-percent of passes allowed for one touchdown after another.   It was all skins could do to try and chase down sprinting receivers, often grabbing one by the back of the shirt to trip him up.   Tempers flared as accusations of cheating were tossed out by each team.   Plays turned into bitter wrestling matches that eventually spoiled the football game.

Many boys, fed up and annoyed, vanished through bright tears in the void's fabric—one breach per individual. Gavin wondered why the game failed to evaporate with the first parting player.   Or the second.   Or the third for that matter.   Visions were supposed to fade out with their dreamers.   Then he realized something sensational.   He'd stumbled across *a communal dream!*   These weren't shadows imagined by one or two brothers, but a large gathering of unrelated dreamers!   Dozens of them!

"How strange," he breathed, marveling at the anomaly.

Then an awful thought caused him a moment's anxiety. What would happen if a group like this approached Dreamland together?   How could a single key keeper safeguard the gates against a crowd?   Such a thing had never happened.   Gavin convinced himself on the spot that it never would.   These dreamers couldn't even cooperate well enough to participate in a successful football game.   For them to manage as a whole to march on Dreamland...

Unlikely.

Wanting to move on, Gavin scanned the expanse for others.   A glance at his back turned up activity afar off.   He quickly headed for it.

Vertically striated cliffs reached toward the sky, grooved and scarred as if dragons had sharpened their claws on the rock for eons.   The cliffs were a solid, high island surrounded by deep waters that appeared like a pool of black ink in the shadows and yet a beautiful ultramarine where the sunlight hit its surface.   The key keeper kept outside the images, knowing one misstep would sink him directly into the sea.

His eyes lifted along the rock face to where voices carried in a downward breeze.   On the ledge stood a slender girl bronzed from head to toe.   A one-piece swimsuit painted her midsection white, reflecting a glare of sunlight off the material.   Three other figures lined up at her back a couple strides off—two young men in swimwear and another girl wearing shorts and a t-shirt.   The bronzed figure brought her arms high and rose up on tiptoe.   She looked poised to dive. With a spring in her jump, she seemed to fly off the cliff's edge.

Gavin put a flat hand to his forehead, shielding his eyes from the sun.   He watched her fall, somersaulting twice with an added twist.   Her body straightened out seconds before slicing cleanly through the water.   She was inarguably skilled at the sport.

The young men took turns performing similarly impressive dives before Gavin tore his attention away.   He scanned the vastness, searching for something else.   But his eyes were drawn back to the cliffs by a terrified scream.   The three divers stood on the ledge again, dripping wet, holding tight to the girl in shorts.   They had her arms and legs secured, threatening to swing her out over the brink.   She was wriggling every muscle in an attempt to break free, screaming and begging for them to set her down on the ground.   Her pleas met no sympathy, only laughter.

The divers counted to three as their hostage shrieked, panicking.   They swung her body forward, backward, and then let her soar into the air on the final frontward thrust. Gavin gasped in horror, only able to observe.   No graceful twists or rolls accompanied her fall, just flailing limbs and fingers scratching at air as if an invisible net existed to grab hold of. Inches before she hit the water, a crack of light erupted in her path and swallowed the girl whole. The nightmare vanished.

Gavin put a hand to his chest, and released the breath he'd held in. He shook his head, jostling his curls, and then turned completely away from the empty spot.

Walking on, his gaze darted in every direction seeking out another dreamer. His footsteps kept to a straight path having a goal of their own in mind, and yet nothing suggested a destination on the horizon. Gavin traveled a distance before it occurred to him where he was headed—where it was he hoped he was headed anyway. Back to the general area where that brown-eyed girl had dreamt.

A vague idea, extremely vague, of the direction he'd traveled to find her the first time guided his steps again. Perhaps she was dreaming in the same spot. Did dreamers appear in the same location twice? Did they keep to a favorite place for every dream? Or did they move about randomly, popping up at chance to invent fantasies wherever they happened to emerge? These were questions Gavin had never considered before.

Roaming for a great deal longer than on his previous visit to the void, Gavin finally admitted he had no idea where he was. He stopped in the middle of nowhere, amply lost. A complete absence of dreamers had him concerned, wondering if it were possible to possess an accurate sense of direction in oblivion. Was this the real reason travelers almost never returned home? Simply because they'd become forever lost?

Gavin reached for his key, fishing it out from beneath his shirt. It wasn't glowing. He wasn't being summoned to the gates, but what if it *did* come to life? How would he find his way back to carry out his calling to safeguard Dreamland?

He swiveled on his heels one-hundred-eighty degrees and hoped retracing his steps (if this truly was the direction he'd come) would take him home. His fingers rubbed in an anxious circular motion on the smooth metallic surface of the key. He scolded himself, regretting his impetuous decision to rush out into a world he knew nothing about. Why had he acted so rashly? Why had he returned to this place despite firm warnings?

Wandering about disoriented, he faced a truth he'd tried to excuse as a curiosity about his mother's origin. To be honest, the cause of his predicament was better blamed on a pair of pretty brown eyes. Gavin longed to gaze into them again, to see that raven-haired girl once more. There was something about the memory of her—something sweet and pleasant—that made him want to seek her out and ask her name. They'd talked so briefly the first time. But this pursuit was proving an impossibility given the immeasurable number of dreamers and the vastness of the void. Whatever had he been thinking?

"Oh, I just wish," he whispered. "How I wish I could find her."

Within his fingers, the key emitted the only source of light around. A shiver of worry trickled like melting ice down the key keeper's spine as he pictured the gates of Dreamland unguarded while he, the sole watchman, had lost himself in the dreamers' void. But then he noticed how the key wasn't glowing in the same radiant manner as usual, rather its metallic structure appeared to glisten as if freshly burnished to make it sparkle. A vision swamped his mind just then—the girl he'd been seeking, kneeling beside a creek with a basket of wet laundry. A clear understanding of her location came to him; he understood which direction to head to the very spot she dreamt.

The lustrous metal went dull in Gavin's hands, but the information disclosed by the key was still his. He stared incredulously at the treasure in his open palm, having learned a secret he'd not known before:

The key to Dreamland has the power to find people with a wish.

The young key keeper grinned, knowing he would never have reason to feel lost again.

Gavin ran all the way to his destination. As the vision had foretold, he found the little raven-haired girl with her pale face and amazing brown eyes scrubbing garments over a washboard in a cold creek. She was dressed in tattered skirts, speaking to a robin perched on a boulder. The bird inclined his head periodically, appearing genuinely interested in her words.

Lacking the courage to approach her, Gavin kept hidden within the shadows of nearby timbers. He was entirely happy to watch the girl dream.

"…and she's not nice at all, oh no! Her daughters aren't as mean as their mother, but they boss me around a lot. 'Do this and do that', they say. But it *is* how the story goes, you know. I am, after all, Cinderella."

"Cinderella," Gavin whispered, thinking he'd discovered her name……until she went on.

"It's not all bad pretending to be Cinderella, because I do get to have a fairy Godmother who grants me wishes and turns pumpkins into carriages and mice into footmen. But don't worry, robin, I don't recall anything from the story about her using magic on birds."

The feathered creature briefly shuddered its wings, then kinked its neck and straightened up, continuing as if listening to the girl's ramblings.

"And my fairy Godmother will turn this ugly old dress into a beautiful gown and then I'll go to the party, which is called a *ball* by royalty, and then I'll dance with a wonderful, handsome prince who will fall in love with me. Oh, and *then* we will be married and live happily ever after! I love fairytales—how they always end that way. I don't see the point of a story ending any other way, do you?"

The robin actually shook its head.

Gavin chuckled to himself, keeping his amusement as hushed as possible.

At that point a commanding female voice shattered the tranquility of the forest. "Cinderella! Cinder-*ella!* Show yourself, you indolent child!"

"That's her," the girl whispered to the bird. "That's my mean step-mother." Quickly rising, she turned to face her approaching mistress. An excuse for why she was at the creek tumbled from her lips.

"I was washing your...uh...underclothes, ma'am." She pointed to the basket of wet laundry as proof. "I'm nearly done."

A stern-faced woman dressed in rich colors and finely-embroidered fabrics rolled her eyes at the scene, making a sound of utter disgust. "Forget that nonsense, Cinderella. We need you at the house. My lovely daughters have been invited to attend a royal ball this very evening! They require your assistance dressing for the occasion. You must wake up, child."

"Excuse me?" the girl asked, looking confused by the woman's last order.

Gavin wondered at the meaning as well.

The pretentious step-mother motioned with her fingers for Cinderella to step away from the creek, making a scoffing

110

sound before speaking again. "Come along child, don't be so slow! There is a ball at the palace tonight, and it is no surprise my sweet dears have been invited. You fell asleep and need to wake up...."

Gavin watched the girl glance at the surrounding woods, her brow taut with confusion. Her eyes scrunched skeptically as if questioning something.

"Cinderella, quit dawdling!" A bejeweled arm shot out, reaching for the disobedient child. The woman vanished before grabbing hold. Yet her voice continued to murmur like a ghost from out of nowhere.

"Get up from the floor and go crawl into your bed."

The key keeper remained focused on the girl, observing the tiniest change in her expression as understanding seemed to slowly seep in.

"Mama?" she mumbled.

Again the mysterious voice softly urged. "Get up. Come on, wake up..."

A blinding streak resembling lightning ripped through the air just then. The brilliance snatched the girl away. Everything else—the creek, the woods, and the robin—faded out of sight. Only Gavin remained. Alone again.

He was about to turn for home when his ears picked up the faintest of conversations; muffled talk once more seemed to come from nowhere. And yet it sounded so terribly near.

"Oh good, you're up. Go hop in bed, baby. It's late."

The key keeper strained an ear to hear. Someone yawned.

"Okay, Mama."

Gavin's jaw dropped, leaving his mouth hanging wide open. It was the same girl! Unmistakably her voice! But no one, nobody, nothing remained to be seen.....where was she?   He knew the answer.   His brown-eyed dreamer had crossed over into her own world.   She was gone.   But how was it possible to hear her voice even now?   Could it be their worlds existed near to one another?   Unseen and yet close by?

It must be so!

His heart thrummed excitedly in his chest as he comprehended an incredible secret.

In truth, only a thin curtain separates Dreamers from Dreamland.

Chapter Ten
The First One

Balanced on the highest beam of a sailing ship, Gavin kept his body close to the main top-mast, trying to appear one with the pole.   The cover of night served him well as a black cloak, concealing his figure from skyward glances.   Far below on the deck of *The Red Dagger*, crew hands saw to a variety of ship's duties by lantern light.   As the night wore on, these weary men began to disperse, retiring below to feast, drink, and sink into idleness.

The captain stood at the helm, not necessarily steering his vessel so much as resting himself on the wheel. Moonlight painted a long streak of luminous white over calm waters. Once the last deck hand disappeared into the galley— after securing ropes and inspecting pulleys—Gavin peered past the beam at his feet. His eyes scrunched in the darkness, searching out the captain.

Drake Blackmont remained at the helm; his arms draped lazily over the wheel, rung through wooden grips. The notorious pirate closed his eyes and breathed in a bouquet of salty sea air. A contented grin crept across his face.

The key keeper made up his mind to lower himself to the deck by rope. His aim was to drop within the shadows and then silently sneak up behind the captain, maintaining an element of surprise. Preparing to act on his plan, a raspy voice rose up, freezing the boy mid-move.

"Climb on down, laddy. Tis only you and me now."

Gavin groaned to himself, realizing his attempt at invisibility hadn't fooled that shrewd, old pirate. He gave up the need to work stealthily, and reached for a secure line. Holding tight, he let his footing slip off the beam. Gravity swung him out into the night air. The boy scrambled down, dropping onto the deck. He stepped into the moonlight to face the ship's captain.

A smirk twitched at each corner of Drake's mouth. "Back to finish our duel, are you, lad? I do believe 'twas you cowering at sword point when we left off."

"I wasn't cowering," Gavin replied defensively. "I tripped over a coil of rope. And I daresay it wasn't a very honorable move on your part to back me into it."

Drake chuckled derisively. "Bah! Binding yerself to codes of honor does nothing but skewer an otherwise decent swordsman. Fight to win, laddy! Fight to *win!* That there should be yer code! Make use of everything at yer disposal to defeat an opponent."

Gavin's gaze tightened as if he were considering the

pirate's advice. Ultimately, he refused it. "A good man can win honorably, captain."

Drake let his head fall back as he laughed aloud. "He can, laddy, aye, he can! But not near as often as *I* win."

There was no arguing the point. It was a fact the infamous Captain Blackmont never lost a duel. And tonight would be no exception.

Ready and eager to challenge the master, Gavin slapped his thigh and produced a long-blade sword from nothingness. He brandished the weapon in a fancy succession of slashes, jabs, and swishes, his feet vigorously prancing about the deck at the same time.

The pirate captain eyed the boy's performance, clearly more amused than impressed. "I'm a bit confused by yer frolickin', laddy. Were you expecting me to duel or dance with you tonight?"

Gavin ceased his warm up and frowned. "Captain Blackmont, sir, while it may be true you possess the greater skill at sword fighting, *I* have found out something even greater!"

A dark eyebrow perked with interest, waiting for the boy to explain.

"I have secrets. *Incredible secrets* about what truly exists outside the gates! I've been out *there*!"

The pirate captain smirked wryly. "Aye, I see, I see. 'Course, lad, you might find we all have our fair share of......surprising secrets."

Gavin's curls shook as he denied anyone could top the knowledge he'd stumbled across earlier that evening. "Not like mine. I. Know. Things." His eyes grew bigger with every emphasized word.

Drake squinted. He questioned the boy—checking. "You know something about dreamers?"

115

"Yes," the key keeper confirmed. He was beaming, his manner bordering on prideful arrogance. For he was now the keeper of novel secrets as well as the coveted key.

The pirate captain made a suggestion. "Perhaps, laddy, it would be more interesting for us to spar bone for bone tonight."

Gavin furrowed his brow, not understanding.

"You know.....the bones of skeletons." Drake waited for the boy to catch on, but he continued to look clueless.

"In yer closet," Drake prompted. He waited, brow lifted expectantly.

"What skeletons?" Gavin finally asked.

The old pirate rolled his eyes. "Secrets! Those secrets you keep like skeletons in yer closet! Bly me!"

"Oh. *Ooooohh!*"

"Daft sprog," Drake grumbled under his breath.

"Hey! I can spar with bones," Gavin declared, "and blades as well. In fact, I can do both at once!"

"Aye, can ye lad?" The captain grinned wide. "I accept that challenge! Yer skill and yer best secrets against mine."

Gavin swiftly extended his blade, pointing it at the pirate's chest. "But no lies, sir. Only the *truth*."

Drake Blackmont dipped his head as a gesture of compliance. "All truth, laddy."

"You swear to it?"

"Aye. That is my *one* veritable fault, you know. I have a painfully honest tongue." Drake grinned in a manner that opposed his sincerity, but he was taken at his word.

Swifter than a blink, the captain had his rapier drawn and its tip pressed against Gavin's chest, having shoved the key keeper's blade aside in the process. "I expect nothing but truthful words from yer lips as well."

A bit startled by the pirate's speed, Gavin swallowed hard. He nodded briskly. "Yes, sir."

Satisfied, the captain stepped back, allowing the boy an opportunity to prepare himself. Drake wiped at his mustache and placed a hand behind him. His rapier he held pointed toward the starlit sky. His eyes remained on the young key keeper who inhaled deeply, filling both lungs with a breath of salty sea air.

Gavin exhaled slowly, restoring his confidence and nerve. It was understood as challenger he would make the first move which included tossing out the first bone, so to speak. In other words, he was obliged to reveal a secret.

The young man shuffled forward and lunged, aiming for the heart. The strike was impeded and a second swatted aside as well. Such casual parries made it appear an easy exercise in blocking for the experienced pirate. While making every effort to slip past Drake's defenses, Gavin spoke about his recent adventure.

"I went to the dreamers' void—beyond the guardians' forest and further on. The emptiness is like nothing I've ever experienced, and yet I found life out there."

Drake circled his blade, entangling Gavin's sword and forcing it high aside. The fighting paused briefly for a question.

"What, dare I ask, motivated a bright, young lad like yerself to wander out in the middle of that bleak wasteland?"

Gavin considered his answer, choosing the safest excuse. "Travelers roam the void. A traveler spoke in parliament recently."

"Aye, tis so, but travelers are known to be madmen. Even the whisperers agree to that. Yer no loon, are you lad?"

Gavin pushed away, freeing his hindered blade. "No, I am not mad. And neither is my father, yet he too has been out there."

The pirate nodded his awareness of the fact.   "That he has.   Aye, that he has."

A series of rapid strikes was attempted by the key keeper, continuing the duel.   Drake parried every blow, but not without retreating a few paces.

"I've learned astounding things about the very dreamers I've been sworn to ward off."

"Tell me, laddy, what do you know?"

Gavin wielded his sword high and brought it down hard—a vertical chop to the head.   The captain merely sidestepped the swipe, raising his eyebrows to communicate a desire for the boy to go on divulging secrets.   Gavin brought his sword horizontal again, checking his balance at the same time.

"Dreamers usually appear alone, surrounded by shadows of their own making; although, it's not uncommon for siblings to dream together now and then—I see that often. But hear this—complete strangers can share in a dream.   Not just one or two individuals, but tens of them!   Perhaps even tens of tens uniting to manipulate one common fantasy!"

Drake cut the air horizontally—a shot to the throat. His rapier was met by Gavin's long blade, colliding edge to edge.   It was a contest of strength as one sword struggled in opposition to the other.   The combatants continued their conversation, speaking through gritted teeth.

"So you're telling me that a crew of scalawags skippered by a clever captain like myself could sail a ship across the void if that crew were to keep a shared dream alive indefinitely?"

"Yes, sir," Gavin grunted, struggling against Drake's strength.

"They could sail right up to Dreamland, could they not.

lad?"

"Possibly," the boy groaned.

"And, quite possibly, a determined pirate might even steer his vessel clean over the borders of Dreamland with ne'er a soul to stop him."

Beads of sweat trickled from beneath Gavin's curly bangs. He dug down deep for extra muscle to hold back his rival. "*I* would stop him."

"Would you now, laddy? Take on an entire ship by yer lonesome? Aye, that there's an interesting notion." Drake sliced sideways unexpectedly, putting a swift end to the standoff.

Gavin caught himself from falling forward at the sudden loss of opposing force. He brought his sword up to have it tapped nonchalantly by the pirate's blade.

"Tell me what else you know, key keeper. Spill it."

The young man retreated by a stride, sizing up the situation again. He obliged the captain and shared his next secret.

"Dreamers appear in the same area of the void more than once. I think they have preferred spots they keep to."

"Aye." The captain nodded, twirling the hilt of his blade in his hand.

"And more often than not their dreams are disturbing. Even nightmarish."

Drake nodded again. "Aye, lad. Dreamers often play out their fears. Yet some do the reverse and dream in hopes of escaping their fears. It's all dependent upon the dreamer."

"Yet everything vanishes in the end—the dreamers and their shadows."

"Tis so, laddy. They return to their own world." The rapier rose to gesture between them. "That is no secret to either of us."

"Yes, yes, but did you know that in reality dreamers don't go far at all?"

"You don't say. Did you follow one, lad? Did you cross over to the other side?"

The key keeper overreacted to the question, seemingly aghast by the possible charge accompanying it. "No! No, of course not! That would be.....completely irresponsible! Downright negligent! Who...who would guard the gates of Dreamland if I were to vanish? I might get stuck there with no way back!"

The pirate captain laughed lowly. "Getting back's as easy as closing yer eyes, lad. Don't worry about that none."

Intrigue brought the young man to a standstill. "Honest?"

Drake winked. "Truthful lips, remember? My one veritable curse."

Gavin nodded. "I believe you. I do. Because I know dreamers exist much closer to us than anyone in parliament realizes. Their world is barely separated from ours by something as thin as a drape. You can't see them, but.....well...."

"But what, lad?"

"Well, this girl.....she vanished before my eyes. I could still hear her voice, though, as clearly as if she were right there, invisible. I could *hear* her, Captain, she was talking to someone. That's how I know dreamers aren't far from us."

"Aye, boy, that is a fact." Drake Blackmont's lips twisted into a devilish grin, and his shrewd eyes scrunched narrowly. He brought his sword to an en garde position and announced, "Now, I believe it's time for me to spill my own bones at yer feet. Don't be surprised that yer secrets are no secret to me."

Gavin raised his sword and took a sideways stance in response to the captain's move. He prepared for a real fight and some surprising truth. It was all the young man could do to parry one strike after another, ducking and retreating as Drake advanced on him like an inescapable sunrise. The boy's ears remained alert from start to finish.

"There was a time in Dreamland's history when no wall or key keeper existed to protect it. Only a forest bordered the land back then. A forest without shadow monsters to scare off roaming dreamers."

"No guardians? But who kept the dreamers away?"

"No one, laddy. At that time no one worried about dreamers. Few wandered far from the void and those who did proved agreeable sorts, easily convinced by whisperers to return home. Parliament had no fear of the rare trespasser until the day the first one refused to turn away from Dreamland. And, aye, he was a right scoundrel if ever they'd met one!"

Gavin scuttled backwards and jumped up on the heightened stern to escape a slicing blade. He ducked behind the ship's wheel to avoid Drake's reach. Eyes and ears wide open, the key keeper listened intently as a shocking tale unraveled.

"A curious dreamer stumbled across this magical world purely by accident. And, being the bright fella he was, it took him no time to figure out that imagining a thing made it all too real in this crazy place. The whisperers tried to ward him off, lure him outside the borders, but he'd have none of it! He wished them away and then wished himself a ship and a fine crew to beat all crews he'd ever captained in his own world. He made himself king of the pirates! But a longing for the companionship of his real crew drove him to wander home. There he awoke, weak and near death. He shared his strange discovery with those few hands who'd remained faithful to him as captain while he'd been unconscious. And wisely, they believed his outlandish tale."

"But he didn't stay with them?"

"Aye, no, for the man was too near death. He'd suffered severe battle wounds—lost precious pints o' blood—before stumbling into Dreamland. For days his body had lain unconscious and undernourished, other than trickles of water poured down his throat by a loyal cabin boy. The Grim Reaper was standing at his door, demanding he give up the ghost. But that cunning captain had found a way to cheat death. For he'd discovered a land of miracles! *Dreamland!"*

Gavin's face tightened with concern as he took in more of the story. He continued to parry every jab thrust through gaps in the wheel.

"The crew was convinced to follow their captain on a dream quest. Everyone slept aboard the pirate ship that night.......ne'er to wake again. But it proved no matter to those scalawags, for they were guided into a magical world where death has no grasp on a man's soul. They sailed into Dreamland on a mighty vessel, floating through the clouds without hindrance, anywhere and everywhere they desired! Such immutable freedom at a buccaneer's command! You can imagine how the men went wild, causing havoc and harassing the locals to no end. Needless to say, these pirate folk became a nasty thorn in parliament's side. 'Twas not only the whisperers but most citizens of Dreamland who demanded the newcomers be banished. "

"But you can't banish a person from Dreamland. They must choose to leave."

"Aye. And that there was parliament's pickle."

"So what did they do? How did they get those foul

122

pirates to go home?"

Drake withdrew his blade and grinned before responding—a clever and devious twist to his lips. "They ne'er did, lad. And they ne'er will."

Gavin's face shifted through a range of emotions as he considered Drake's words: from confusion, to wonder, to a sudden understanding that led to sheer shock.

"You? You were the….the…."

"The foul pirate. A dreamer. The first one to invade Dreamland and stake it as home."

"But you're…..you've been..…"

"A legend? An icon? Every lad's unequaled champion?" The captain hopped up on the heightened stern, moving cautiously forward, holding his stunned listener captive with exposed secrets.

"I've had many, many long years to weave my story into what I wish it to be. I've eased up since those first days—survived every harrowing adventure a seadog could imagine. But 'twas *me* who sparked parliament to surround Dreamland in stone walls and fill the forest with daunting guardians. 'Twas *me* to stir up such chaos as to create a need for a locked fortress and a vigilant key keeper. 'Twas *me* who instilled fear in yer whimsical world."

Gavin froze, stunned. His countenance tensed with incredulity. His eyes grew wide and bewildered as every breath intensified. The tip of a rapier threatened the young man before he sufficiently found his wits. But even when he realized his precarious state, his eyes merely glanced down at the threatening blade. He squinted up at a famous swordsman who suddenly looked darkly altered. The nefarious side of this pirate defined him entirely now. He was an outsider. A trespasser. An intruder!

Remembering his mother was all those things too,

Gavin felt a pang of guilt for despising the man so intensely. But their circumstances were entirely different. His mother had been *invited* into Dreamland. She was a decent soul who strived to make their world a better place. Drake had painted himself a villain plaguing the land! He and his crew would've suffered banishment had such a thing proved possible. He was a scourge to Dreamland! At least—at one time he had been.

The captain held his sword at Gavin's throat and spoke as if he could read every thought passing through the boy's mind.

"I brought *treasure* to Dreamland, laddy. Things your docile and unassuming people didn't esteem as valuable until they got a good, hearty taste of it."

"Treasure? You call mayhem and fear *treasure?*"

"Aye, I do. What I gave this world was spirit! A yearning for adventure! A craving for challenges! Anticipation, laddy! Ambition and drive and hope! Generations of young ones have possessed more fire in their souls simply because Captain Blackmont came along! Dreamland is better off for the scars I carved into this land." Drake tapped Gavin's chin with the tip of his sword. "And you, key keeper....you've *me* to thank for yer mighty calling."

A stare down locked the two in a silent and serious moment until a crooked grin began to inch across Drake's face. A low chuckle had barely begun to rise from his throat when Gavin batted the pirate's rapier aside and lunged forward. He aimed for the heart. The sight of scarlet startled the boy— blood oozing from where his sword had actually hit!

His eyes grew big, understanding what he'd done. But something had prevented him from more than pricking the pirate's flesh. Gavin was certain it wasn't loyalty to preserve Drake's undefeated reputation; he would've speared the rouge had he been able to.

Feeling surprisingly cold and weak, the young man looked down at himself. The golden hilt of a rapier stuck out from below his ribs. Drake hadn't failed to pierce him after all. That devious pirate had won again.

Gavin fell to the ground, overwhelmed by regret.....or relief.....he wasn't sure.

Then he felt a boot at his shoulder, jostling him. "Get up, lad."

Gavin opened his eyes to look up at the captain rubbing his fingers in blood.

"I believe you scratched me. Were you actually planning on running me through, laddy?"

The key keeper swallowed without answering.

Drake laughed aloud and reached down to reclaim his sword. He then snatched the boy up by the collar. "She must be a pretty thing to have you this fired up. That lass has got you behaving carelessly."

So he was blaming the raven-haired girl—assuming what happened was because of her. Gavin felt his cheeks betray him, flushing. He muttered a reply. "She would never be mistaken for a foul pirate, that's for sure."

The captain laughed aloud. All humor ended when a sudden radiance emanated from the key, beckoning its owner.

"Get along, laddy. Best not be lettin' scalawags like me inside these gates."

"Aye," Gavin agreed. And the young man scurried off.

Chapter Eleven
A New Friend

She was all dressed in red, swathed by a long, hooded cloak that covered her raven hair, protecting her from the chilly air. Her feet kept on a dirt path partially hidden by discarded autumn leaves. Laced boots reached well above her ankles, the kind lined with soft, warm fur. Her arms swung at her sides, one hand clutching at a basket of aromatic treats.

Gavin stood within the trees, observing her from the shadows. He watched the basket rise to her nose as she closed her eyes to sniff at its contents. A smile told him it smelled delicious, but she didn't open the container to pinch off a sample. Instead, the basket lowered to swing at her side as it had previously done.

All at once the air was filled with soft singing—a sweet, merry tune comprised of ludicrous lyrics. It was impossible not to grin at the words.

> *"Rainbows paint the sky 'til the sun melts their colors.*
> *Swinging in the wind, whiskered cattails purr.*
> *The pigs gallop by and snort at the moon,*
> *While frogs kiss the lizards and princesses too."*

The young key keeper left his shadowy hiding place and stepped onto the trail. He was fairly sure this raven-haired creature had no idea the path she traveled led straight to the front gates of Dreamland. The singing stopped abruptly, and the girl paused in mid step. Her brown eyes widened, spotting him.

Gavin was draped in a cloak similar to the one this dreamer wore, only it was black in color to match his usual choice in wardrobe. At that point the two stood still as statues, staring at one another across the way.

When the girl didn't move, Gavin summoned her near with his fingers. His heart thrummed as she obeyed, stepping up close to him. Her young stature was much shorter than his tall, wiry form. Gavin regarded her prettiness—pale cheeks, pink lips, inquisitive eyes. Fascinated by her, he longed to know her name.

"Who are you?" he asked. He heard the girl utter the same question at the same time.

Cocking his head, he claimed, "I asked you first."

"No you didn't," she protested, shaking her red-hooded head. "I asked you at the same time you asked me."

Gavin grinned at her insistence. It was hard for him not to chuckle. "Well then, I suppose we'll have to go with girls first.'" His grin widened into a white smile.

The girl gestured to herself. "I'm Little Red Riding Hood."

He recognized the name of a fairytale character and groaned under his breath at not having discovered this dreamer's real name.

"Actually," she confessed almost immediately, "I'm not really Red Riding Hood. My name is Annabelle, but I'm pretending to be her because......well......because this is my dream and that's what I wish to dream about."

Oh glorious day! He'd learned her name! Annabelle! Annabelle! What a perfectly sweet sound was his utterance of.....*Annabelle!*

It was work for the young key keeper to prevent his elation from showing. He twisted his expression into a serious look. "That's what you want to dream about? Some girl in a red cloak?"

"It's better than dreaming about some boy in a drab, black cloak," Annabelle defended.

Gavin looked down at himself. "I'm only wearing this black cloak because you're wearing that red one."

"You're copying me?"

"Not entirely."

They stopped to stare suspiciously at one another. It was quiet through the long gaze. Leaves rustled overhead while a breeze managed to sweep beneath Gavin's hood, tousling his brown curls. He spoke up first.

"Annabelle."

"Yes?"

"I like your name."

"You do?" Pink lips grinned involuntarily. The girl bit down on them. Her brown eyes glistened in a strange mix of astonishment and hope.

The look was enough to steal Gavin's heart. It made him want to stay with her, to play with this outsider forever. The unexpected butterflies in his chest produced an awkward feeling—uncomfortably potent. He quickly changed the subject, inviting himself to share in her fantasies.

"I don't care for your dream, though. It's boring. Let's do something else."

Sweet Annabelle turned defensive. "You don't even know where my dream was headed. I'm off to Grandmother's house with this basket of goodies."

Gavin's dark eyes flickered to the basket and then back to the red-hooded girl. He sniffed once at the air. "Boring."

Annabelle's gaze narrowed slightly as she revealed the kicker to her dream. "My grandmother won't be there when I get to her house..."

"Can we eat those goodies then?" Gavin asked, interrupting.

"No!" Small hands moved the basket protectively behind the red cloak. "I need these goodies to feed to the wolf that'll be lying in my grandmother's bed. He's probably already eaten her by now."

The key keeper's eyes grew wide. Did this girl just talk of his favorite pastime? Being eaten by a big bad wolf!

"Not so boring?" Annabelle asked with a tiny hint of smugness.

"That depends," Gavin said, once again trying to keep his elation disguised. "When we get there, is this wolf going to eat you too?"

The red-hooded dreamer looked suddenly worried. "I don't think so."

Gavin tapped his foot against the ground as if irritated by her answer. "What do you mean you don't think so? Haven't you thought this out?"

130

"Well, um," she hemmed, "this isn't actually my story. It's a book my teacher read to our class."

"So how does it end?"

Annabelle admitted sheepishly, "She hasn't read the ending yet, but it probably ends like every other fairytale."

Gavin's foot stopped its tapping. "How's that?"

"Well, the evil villain is defeated, and the hero runs off with the princess and lives happily ever after."

The key keeper rolled his eyes. "Bor~ing. I think the girl should be eaten by the wolf."

"But that can't happen," she argued. "Nobody would care for a story like that."

"Why not?"

"Because no one wants to read about a little girl who dies in the end. It's too sad. It's not how fairytales go. And besides, I really don't want to be eaten by a wolf. It might hurt." Her pretty face tightened with concern. She looked genuinely worried this dark young man might force her to be eaten.

"What if I let him eat me? When he's done, we can sit down and share those goodies in your basket."

The girl thought about it for a second, then shrugged one shoulder. "Okay."

Happy and content, Gavin pulled back his hood, uncovering a thick mess of brown curls. He turned and stepped along the trail. His dark eyes sparkled, peering over a shoulder at his new friend. He planned to learn everything there was to know about her. Consequently, he would gain knowledge of her world in the process. Who needed second-hand reports from Drake or his father or the whisperers when he could go to the source directly?

"Come on, Annabelle. That hungry wolf isn't going to wait around forever."

The raven-haired girl hustled up beside him. Looking past a rim of red fringe above her eyes, she stared at his dimpled profile.

"What's your name?" she finally asked the boy.

His pointed chin lifted proudly with his answer. He didn't hesitate telling her the truth. "I'm Gavin. Key keeper of Dreamland."

~ The End

In loving memory of
Annabelle Fancher

Some live for their own joy and pleasure.

Some live to ease the burdens of others.

Then there are those who seem to exist
for pain's sake only;
that in the end,
the wrathful fire sent
to consume their oppressors
will be justified.

-Richelle E. Goodrich

About the Author

Richelle E. Goodrich is native to the Pacific Northwest, born in Utah but raised in Washington State. She lives with her husband and three boys somewhere in a compromise between city and country settings. Richelle graduated from Eastern Washington University with bachelor's degrees in Liberal Studies and Natural Science / Mathematics Education. She loves the arts—drama, sketching, painting, literature—and writes whenever opportunity presents itself. This author describes herself beautifully in the following quote:

"I like bubbles in everything. I respect the power of silence. In cold or warm weather, I favor a mug of hot cocoa. I admire cats— their autonomy, grace, and mystery. I awe at the fiery colors in a sunset. I believe in deity. I hear most often with my eyes, and I will trust an expression before any accompanying comment. I invent rules, words, adventures, and imaginary friends. I pretend something wonderful every day. I will never quit pretending."
    -Richelle E. Goodrich

Read the book that inspired
Secrets of a Noble Key Keeper...

Dandelions: The Disappearance of Annabelle Fancher
by Richelle E. Goodrich

What does a child do when life hurts? She dreams up a hero.
~ A childhood trial of survival.
~ Realism and fantasy beautifully intertwined.

This fictional tale is a suspenseful, human-interest account detailing the harsh reality endured by young Anna. It tenderly acquaints the reader with a lonely young girl and shares her courage facing adversity. Many of the events were taken from the lives of actual people.

Annabelle Fancher lives with her mother and her often-absent, alcoholic father. When he's not on the road, his presence at home instills heightened anxiety in his wife and daughter—fear caused by years of drunken cruelty. Annabelle copes with her circumstances by escaping into storybooks where she dreams characters to life from popular fairytales. There in her dreams she manages to form make-believe moments of happiness.

School is the only place she interacts socially, where a few individuals suspecting her circumstances attempt to reach out to the quiet child; however, it is an imagined friend whom she turns to repeatedly for comfort and kindness. But when his ghostly form appears during waking hours—his voice augmenting the hallucination—it becomes a struggle for Annabelle to keep reality and pretend from blurring boundaries. Her choice, it seems, is to happily succumb to madness or embrace her cruel reality.

Made in the USA
San Bernardino, CA
20 May 2015